HER LAST WORD

BROTHERHOOD PROTECTORS WORLD

STACEY WILK

Twisted Page Press LLC

BROTHERHOOD PROTECTORS

ORIGINAL SERIES BY ELLE JAMES

To Lisa, Robin, and Ellen
Our children introduced us. Your big hearts and bigger
attitudes made us lifelong friends.

CHAPTER 1

SHE HAD ten minutes to escape out the back door. She needed three. Cheyenne Locklear grabbed the computer, shoved it in her backpack, and charged out into the night. The air was thick, and the temperature had been at an all-time high for July. Lightning cracked open the Montana sky and gave her enough light to high-tail it into the woods and leave her house and her life behind.

Her lungs protested as her feet pounded the uneven ground and she dodged the thin- trunked trees. She needed a faster way to flee than by foot from racehorse owner Tucker Gray and his merry men. Even in the middle of her crisis, she snickered at her own bad humor.

A horse would do just fine to take her to the county police, and she knew where to find a horse at this time of night. The owner would be mad she took it without asking, but there wasn't time to ask. She'd explain it all later, and he'd understand because it was her. If someone else took his horse, he might kill them. Quint Porter had killed before and for a lot less. His ranch butted up against her property, and she could sneak up on the barn.

Tucker and whoever he sent to kill her would be at her place soon. It wasn't enough to ruin her reputation as a veterinarian because she wouldn't commit a crime for him. He wanted her out of the picture entirely, and he would have succeeded if she hadn't noticed the twitch in the sheriff's eye when she told him what she knew about the practices of Cactus Ranch. The man never could play poker, or stay out of Tucker Gray's pocket. Her suspicions were confirmed when her security system announced someone had come onto the property. That's when the clock started ticking.

She tripped over a fallen tree and face-planted in slimy leaves. Her backpack went flying. She scrambled to her feet and grabbed the bag. She was almost there.

The trees spaced out, and the grass spread out in front of her. The Weston Ranch was a hundred acres. The horse barns were on this side of the property. The head rancher's house was nearby. Quint didn't own the ranch. He worked for Ty Weston as the head rancher and had been employed there since his release from prison. Quint was good with the horses, and the men on the ranch respected him. Or feared him.

The guest ranch was a mile away. No one but Quint

would hear her in the barn, not that she wanted him to hear anything. She had to hope he was somewhere else on the property tonight. Maybe playing cards with the other cowboys and losing his shirt. She'd return the horse once she made it to safety with a note and six-pack of Cold Smoke Scotch Ale. That used to be his favorite beer.

She skidded to a stop outside the barn and took a deep breath. Her heart needed to slow down, or the horses would sense her nerves. If they acted up and made noise, Quint would come running. She unlatched the barn door and slid it to the side. The last thing she needed after escaping Tucker Gray was to run head-first into Quint Porter.

HOW MANY MORE TIMES WOULD HE have to tell Hank Patterson no? Quint shifted from one foot to the other and shoved his hands in his jean's pockets. They stood on Quint's front porch. It was late and he was ready to throw back a beer alone. He held Hank's gaze and hoped he would understand there was no changing his mind. "Thank you, sir, but I'm still not interested in your offer. I like my job on the ranch just fine."

Hank removed his white cowboy hat and rubbed a hand over his buzz-cut. "Quint, you're wasting your time working this ranch. You're good at what you do, but you have skills that would benefit the Brotherhood

Protectors and everyone we guard. Ty agrees, and he's ready to let you go so you can come work for me. I'm overloaded with cases. I need your help."

"Come on man, my team needs a third," Jax Montero said. Jax always came with Hank when they tried to persuade him to work for the Brotherhood. Jax was a good guy, and someone he would want to work with – in another life.

"Ever since I busted my wife's uncle and changed the face of the Supreme Court, requests for Lincoln and me to be bodyguards have been blowing up my phone. We need another man on our team to help us out so I can take a vacation again." Jax held up his phone as if the calls were coming in at that minute.

Hank smirked. "Montero, this isn't about you. What do you say, Quint? I will double what Ty pays you."

"Ty pays pretty well, sir. You sure you can afford me?" He hoped a little humor might lighten the mood.

The extra money would be nice to sock away when his body was too old to wrangle horses, but he didn't need it. He lived on the ranch, and the ranch met all his needs. "Give the job to another vet who needs it more than I do." A man like him, a man with his past, didn't deserve to work for the Brotherhood Protectors.

He wanted a former service member who couldn't find employment because of an injury or PTSD to work for Hank. Hank located good men and women who had returned to civilian life and made them part of the Brotherhood Protectors. They were useful again. He had his purpose right on the ranch.

"I want your skills and your work ethic. Think about it. The offer always stands. I've said this to you before, Quint. I don't care about your past. I know it wasn't your fault." Hank adjusted his hat.

"My answer is still the same, sir. Thank you, but no thank you." He didn't want to guard anyone. He wanted to keep his head down, stay out of trouble, and do his job. Since his release from prison, he'd been able to do just that.

Hank held out his hand. "It would be an honor to add you to my team."

When was the last time anything he did was honorable? And when did someone else think so? He gripped Hank's hand and shook. "Thank you."

"We're playing poker at my house Friday night if you want to get to know Linc. Come on by." Jax held his hand out too.

"I'm not much of a poker player." He shook again.

"Let's go, Montero. I think you have diapers to change. Night, Quint."

"Good night."

The two men sauntered over to Hank's pickup with laughter filling the space around them and drove away.

Finally.

Quint grabbed a beer from the fridge and settled in the rocking chair on his front porch. It was a perfect night. The humidity was low; the sky was filled with stars, and he was alone. He closed his eyes. His mind searched for the demons, but tonight he didn't search hard. It had been a good day. He broke a new stallion for Ty. They took out a pack of guests for a ride, and no one got hurt. His men were reliable. The demons could come back tomorrow because they would. He was still Quint Porter.

The clapping of hooves broke the silence. He sat straighter. A horse whinnied. He pushed out of the chair. No one should be on this side of the property.

"Yah," a voice said.

He ran for the barn.

A female rider and his horse, Fly Me to the Moon, barreled past him. *His horse.* Who the hell would steal his horse? Because he didn't have one female working on the ranch at the moment that didn't have a job inside so it wasn't an employee of the ranch out for a ride. The inside workers would have asked first.

"Hey." He ran and shouted. "Come back here."

They kept going. Right into the woods. The only place they could head was up the mountain or into the river.

"Fuck." He turned on his heel and ran for his ATV.

He jumped on and took off. He followed in the direction they went, but if this thief knew anything about horses, then she could have gone in many directions, and he'd be hard-pressed to find them.

And if she didn't know a damn thing about how to ride, then she could hurt his horse, and that would not

6

bode well for her. He might, for the first time in his life, not care that hitting a woman was wrong.

The ATV's light helped him dodge trees. He didn't need a crash. No one knew where he was. They wouldn't find him for hours or maybe days. A few cheers would rise up at his disappearance, but he wasn't ready to die.

The air blew against his face and swelled his shirt behind him as he raced uphill. He could not hear the horse gallop over the sound of the engine. She would be able to hear him coming up on her. He didn't know if that was a good thing or a bad one. Another horse might have been better transportation, but he didn't have time to saddle up.

The woman had saddled his horse. He'd seen that much. Okay, she knew what she was doing. That was good, but if she did anything to his horse... he let his thoughts disappear. He needed to find them first.

He bumped over uneven ground. The smell of pine scented the air. He didn't see the horse. If she was an experienced rider, knew how to find a horse and steal it, then maybe she knew the terrain as well. It was a shot, and he had to take it.

He banked left and hit the gas. The trees would spread out to a clearing before the running stream. If she followed that stream about two miles, she'd come to the road. The road would be the quickest way anywhere. And where was this woman going on his fucking horse?

He hit the brakes. The ATV skidded. His ass came up off the seat. He gripped the handlebars and forced his feet back to the footrest before he landed on his head. His horse trotted toward him without the rider.

"Fuck." He jumped off. "You okay, Moon?" He took the reins and checked him over. "Go on now." Moon went down the hill without a care. He knew his way back to the barn. At least the horse wasn't hurt, but something might have spooked him. He doubted the rider dismounted and went on foot.

"Where is she?" He grabbed a flashlight and a rope from his pack. He'd hog-tie her if he had to and drag her back to the sheriff.

The moon offered some light, but he was still in the trees, and the tall pines had branches reaching for the sky.

He tripped over something but righted himself. He pointed the beam on a backpack and not a body. A long breath escaped his lips. The backpack looked new. She couldn't be far.

"Ma'am, are you out here? Are you hurt? Just tell me where you are, and I'll come to you."

She could pounce. It might be nice to have a gun about now in case she was crazy or on drugs, but he would never handle a firearm again. He took a few steps and stopped.

A slight woman lay on her side. Her head was bent at a strange angle, and her legs curled up as if she was asleep. Her long, dark hair covered her face.

"Ma'am?"

He nudged her foot with his toe. Nothing. She had no reason to play possum except he had been fast on her heels with a noisy vehicle, giving his location away at every second. She would be taking a big risk like this. If she was smart enough to steal a horse, she would be smart enough to want the ATV instead. She didn't have a gun strapped to her. He nudged her leg this time. Still nothing.

He squatted down and moved her hair away from her face. Blood ran from a gash on her forehead. The cold hand of dread reached into his chest and froze his lungs. This wasn't any woman. This was Cheyenne Locklear, or hot Doc Lock as his men referred to her. Which he hated because he didn't like her being spoken about that way. Even if she was beautiful. Her looks didn't matter. Rumor had it she was making mistakes and hurting the animals she treated. The rumors were strong enough to empty out her waiting room. He should've asked her if those rumors were true, but he kept quiet when she came to the ranch to check on the horses. Were those rumors making her run?

He hunted for a pulse, and came up with a weak one. At least she wasn't dead, but someone would think he did this for no other reason than he was capable.

He blotted her head with his handkerchief then reached for his phone to call Ty, but didn't have it. That left only two choices. He could leave her here and pretend he never saw her take his horse or he could go back to his house, grab that beer, and mind his own business.

There was another choice, but he didn't like it. He could scoop her up and take her to the hospital. He would deposit her by the emergency room door and walk away before anyone saw him. At least she would get the help she needed, and she'd be safe from whoever had her scared.

He grabbed her backpack and stowed it. He lifted her with care and settled her in front of him on the ATV so he could keep an arm around her small waist and stop her from falling. Her head rested against his shoulder. She smelled like moonflowers, lemon and exotic.

His experience taught him sometimes blame came even if it wasn't deserved. He hadn't meant to kill anyone in the bar that night, but he wasn't going to allow a man to hit a woman. What had Cheyenne stealing horses and running? She fled late at night for a reason. If someone was coming for her and followed her here, it would do him good to be as far away from her as possible or risk getting caught up in something he didn't want to be a part of. He followed the stream to the road.

Maybe she hadn't hurt those animals like the rumors said. It would be a shame if her career was ruined over a lie, though. She was a good woman. Too good for him. She had said as much, and she was right.

He stopped the ATV deep in the parking lot of the

10

hospital and carried her to the emergency room door. He held her close to keep her from moving too much in his arms. Her soft curves pressed into his lines and angles. She fit against him as if she was meant to, and he shook that thought away like a bird in flight. She was not for him.

The hospital was quiet this time of night. Relief pushed him forward. The ambulance bay was empty. No one was outside. He eased her down onto the bench by the door and brushed her hair away from her face. He took off his flannel shirt and draped it over her like a blanket. It wasn't much, but it was something. Hopefully, Cheyenne wasn't outside alone for long.

"What the fuck am I doing?" He scooped her back up and walked inside.

A sigh escaped his lips. He didn't know the woman behind the counter. She jumped up as he approached. "What happened?"

He placed Cheyenne on a gurney next to the registration desk. "She got tossed."

He turned on his heel and walked back into the night.

"Wait," the woman called after him.

So much for wanting to keep his head down and stay out of the way. It had been a good ride until now because whether he liked it or not, Cheyenne Locklear just forced him out of his quiet life and into trouble's path.

CHAPTER 2

QUINT POURED his first cup of strong black coffee for the day and turned on the television to the local news. He wanted the forecast. He could check his phone, except this weather guy almost always got it right. The sun wasn't up yet, but the horses and the cattle would need tending. He liked to get a head start on things. Running this part of the ranch was his responsibility. It gave him a purpose.

He hadn't slept much because thoughts of Cheyenne kept him tossing and turning. He resisted the urge to call the hospital and find out if she was okay. Word would spread if something bad happened to the local vet. He'd know something by the day's end. He'd done his good deed, and he wouldn't say a word about her taking his horse. She had enough problems on her hands.

Breaking news flashed on the television screen

beside the morning anchor. The scene switched to outside the hospital and the bench he'd almost left Cheyenne sitting on. Quint turned up the volume and nearly dropped his coffee.

Koda Locklear stood outside the doors flanked by the sheriff and a doctor in his white lab coat. Koda's dark hair stuck up in different directions. Dark circles covered his eyes, and he hadn't shaved. He held a piece of paper in shaking hands. *Missing* scrolled across the bottom of the screen.

"My sister, Doctor Cheyenne Locklear, was brought here last night by a stranger. She had a head injury. The hospital admitted her. By this morning, she'd gone missing." He pressed his fingers into his eyes. "We are looking for any clues to her whereabouts. She may have amnesia and may have left the hospital not understanding where she was. If anyone knows anything at all, please come forward. No one will be arrested if they caused her injuries. I just want her to come back safely. She's all I have left. Thank you." He choked on the last words and broke down.

The sheriff patted Koda on the back and walked him away. The screen switched back to the anchors. Quint turned off the television.

The woman at the desk last night could identify him. If Cheyenne went missing, they would think he had something to do with it. At the very least, he would be questioned about her injuries. He hung his head. He should've left her on the ground by the stream and let someone else stumble upon her.

"Who the fuck are you kidding? You were never going to leave her outside that hospital bleeding like that," he said.

He poured out the coffee and shoved his arms into his shirt. He would need to call Ty and tell him what happened. But he had no proof that he didn't hurt Cheyenne. No one saw her take the horse. His argument that he was trying to take back what was his would not stand up. No one would believe he stumbled upon her already hurt. He could have easily banged her head against a rock or tree. It didn't matter that he didn't have any reason to hurt her. He would always be guilty first.

He fumbled for his phone, but what if Ty didn't believe him? Without Ty backing him up, he wouldn't have a leg to stand on. The sheriff would drag his ass into jail without question.

He ran out of the house. The sun climbed around the mountaintop and pushed the darkness to the side for a softer gray. The cool air licked his skin. The ranch would buzz with activity soon. There wasn't much time. He hurried to the shed and tugged at the door.

One thing inside this shed might prove he didn't hurt Cheyenne or take her from the hospital. He could make the argument he was trying to save his horse. Ty would have to believe him now.

For once in his sorry life, luck could be on his side. He still had her backpack.

He flipped open the storage box on the back of the ATV.

It was empty.

"Are you looking for this?" Cheyenne stepped from behind ladders propped in the corner and held up the backpack.

"Shit. Are you crazy announcing yourself that way? I could have killed you." If she had so much as tapped him on the shoulder, he would have swung first and asked questions later.

The shed was dark. Even as it was, he could only make out her long hair hanging over her shoulders against his flannel shirt. He swallowed the knot in his throat. His shirt hung to her jean-covered knees, and the sleeves were rolled up. It looked good on her.

"I didn't mean to frighten you. I'm sorry about that."

"You could have stayed hidden. I would never have seen you. Why did you show yourself?"

"I need your help."

"Hell, no. Take your bag and go." He turned on his heel but stopped. "Do you know people are looking for you?"

She gave a small laugh. "That's why I stole your horse."

"I mean your brother. He put out a cry for help on channel twelve."

She tilted her chin up and let out a long breath. "I

should have known he would do something like that. He doesn't understand. Will you keep me hidden until the Montana Five Star Race at the end of the week?"

"Lady, you are crazy." He heard enough. "Make sure you're gone when I get back." He would give her ten minutes to take a hike. He'd have to buy himself a new shirt.

"It's your fault the whole town is looking for me."

Her words lassoed his chest and stopped him in his tracks. He should keep his back to her and return to his house for another cup of coffee. Or something stronger. "Why is it my fault? I was minding my own business until you broke into my barn."

"I would have returned your horse. I needed a ride, not a trip to the hospital."

"Then I guess you'd better learn how to ride a horse because when I came up to you, you were knocked out cold."

"You should have left me there."

"I was thinking the same thing." He shifted from one foot to the other.

"You would have left me? Of course, you would. You're Quint Porter."

He stepped forward but stopped. He could be heard just fine from his spot by the door. "Hey, you're the one who just said I should have left you. But I didn't. I brought you to the hospital, remember? Don't go getting mad at me for something I didn't do." If anyone discovered she was on the ranch, they would throw the book at him. "Get off this ranch. I'm not going to jail again."

"I'm sorry. I shouldn't have said that. Your reputation, well…"

"I know what you think of me, what you and everyone else have always thought. Some of it is true, but not everything. I would not have left you to die out in the woods. Now, please go. I have work to do."

The sun broke over the mountain and splashed the day with bold colors. The heat would cook the dirt soon, and the day would smell of sweat, horses, and hard work. He wanted his simple life, and now this woman wearing his shirt had blown it away like a target on the firing range.

"I have nowhere else to go, and you're the only person who knows I was running last night. Now that Koda told the whole town and then some that I'm missing, I have too many people looking for me. I only need a few days. After the race, you'll never have to see me again."

"What are you running from?" He needed to know before he could help her.

"The less you know, the better off you'll be. Will you do it?"

"Quint Porter, you in that shed of yours?" Sheriff Lee's voice came in on the wind.

"Get behind those ladders and don't come out until I come back." He closed the door to the shed and hoped she would listen to him.

"Morning, Sheriff." He shoved his hands in his back pockets.

Sheriff Lee wore a baseball cap with the town emblem embroidered across the front and the standard beige pants with brown shirt. He was tall and wispy, but the sheriff had trained in martial arts. He could snap a man in half. His hand hovered near his gun. He probably didn't want to take any chances this far away from another person. The sheriff didn't trust him. He didn't trust the sheriff, so they were even in his mind.

Quint tried not to smile at the idea he made Sheriff Lee uncomfortable.

"Quint, where were you last night around eleven?"

"Right here."

"Anyone see you?" The sheriff spit on the ground.

"What's this about?" He knew his rights. Had made sure he read enough law books that he could pass the bar if he wanted. Sheriff Lee wouldn't get away with scaring anything out of him.

"Dr. Locklear went missing last night right from her hospital bed. Pretty strange, if you ask me."

He wasn't asking. In fact, he didn't have a whole lot to say on the subject. Hopefully, the sheriff would figure that out soon. He wanted to risk a glance over his shoulder to make sure Cheyenne wasn't standing there, but he kept his gaze locked on the sheriff's. A man with nothing to hide made eye contact.

"Someone fitting your description dropped off Doc Locklear at the hospital and walked out without saying who he was. You wouldn't happen to know anything about that, now would you?"

"I saw her brother on the news this morning. Sounds like whoever took her to the hospital was doing a good deed. I hope you find her, though."

The sheriff narrowed his eyes. "Her brother is pretty upset. We really want her back. You said you were here all alone? You didn't spend any time with the cowboys in their bunkhouse?"

"I never said I was alone."

"Who can I ask to confirm your whereabouts?"

"Am I a suspect?" He held his breath. The sheriff could make his life a living hell if he wanted, and there would be damn little he could do about it. He didn't have a lawyer to call if suddenly he was at the top of the list of people to suspect.

"Should you be?"

As if a criminal would answer yes to that question. He expected a little more from old Sheriff Lee. "I have a ranch to run, and I'm off to a late start. Unless you have something other than a bad description, I suggest you take your investigation elsewhere. Dr. Locklear is important to this town. Everyone will want her found."

"You're an ex-convict. You don't get the same treatment as my law-abiding citizens. Who saw you last night?"

Anger stirred low in his belly. He was a damn law-following citizen and had been every day of his life except for the ten minutes it took to beat the shit out of man abusing his physical power.

He hated what he was about to do. It wasn't a complete lie, but enough of one he didn't like the taste of it in his mouth. He would never have taken advantage this way any other time. Always seemed he found himself in situations where he did something he wouldn't any other time.

"Hank Patterson and Jax Montero were here." The timing was slightly off, but if he guessed right, Hank would vouch for him first then ask questions later. He'd have to tell Hank the whole story about Cheyenne and the horse if he asked. He wouldn't be able to keep Cheyenne completely hidden, but he would never lie to Hank.

The sheriff's eyes widened like tumbleweeds growing in the wind. "That's a pretty impressive crowd you're running with. Does Patterson know your history?"

"You'll have to ask him. Are we through?"

Sheriff Lee adjusted his cap. "For now."

He waited until the sheriff drove away before going back to Cheyenne inside the shed. "Come out here. He's gone."

She stepped around the ladders. The sunlight now spilled in and brightened her tawny skin. Her bottom lip was full, and a bruise had formed on the corner of her mouth. Her striking blue eyes that normally shone against her bronze skin now smoldered with what was either anger or fear. What was this woman up against, and what had he been dragged into?

"What did he say?" She still held the backpack in front of her.

"The woman at the hospital identified me. I just lied to Sheriff Lee about my alibi. Now, you are going to tell me who's after you and why, or I'm going to drag you out into the open because I never lie. Do you hear me? I never lie, and because of you, I just did." He should know better and not get involved. The last time he got involved with a woman who was in trouble, he landed in jail.

But he would never allow a woman to be hurt. No matter what. And that included Cheyenne Locklear who was in over her head and needed some help. People like her didn't go looking for trouble.

"Tell me, Cheyenne."

"How do I know I can trust you?"

"You don't, but once you stole my horse you forced yourself to trust me. If you didn't want to deal with me, you should have broken into someone else's barn."

She hugged her backpack to her chest. "I need to prove Tucker Gray is injecting his horses with steroids before he kills me."

"Why do you think Gray wants to kill you?" It explains why she stole his horse.

"I told on him."

"And you think Gray would hurt his horses for money?"

Tucker owned Cactus Ranch and everyone associated with it in a fifty-mile radius. Except for Ty Weston and his family and of course Hank Patterson. Gray bred and ran race horses and was very good at it. Racing magazines interviewed him and said Gray was what the industry needed. Trainers fell over themselves to work for him. The ladies couldn't keep their hands off of him because money and power were sexy. Except Gray's horses sometimes ended up dead unexpectedly. No one ever proved he was doing something wrong, but Quint didn't believe in coincidences.

"I know he would hurt those horses without a second thought." She dropped her gaze and kicked the dirt.

"How?"

She tilted her chin up. "Because he asked me to do it, and I told him no."

"So, in other words, you're fucked."

"Pretty much."

And now he was fucked too.

CHAPTER 3

CHEYENNE'S PLAN TO escape Tucker only managed to land her in bed with a wolf. Granted, Quint was an attractive wolf, if someone liked a man with his jaw covered in a scruffy beard, always wearing flannel, ripped jeans, boots, and a cowboy hat for every occasion. Which of course, she did. His reputation for anger and violence set her on edge. She had enough problems without tangling with him, but she had seen another side to him before. He wasn't bad to the core. And if she was wrong about him, she would end up dead. Tucker planned on killing her anyway.

"Will you help me?" She cringed at the begging in her voice, but she was out of options.

Once she woke up in a hospital bed a little unsure of how she got there, she had to get out and hide before Tucker found her. He and his men wouldn't go away easily.

She remembered riding Fly Me to the Moon faster than he liked to go. Something scurried in front of their path, and Moon freaked out. She was airborne and then lying in a hospital bed with a gash on her head. Her backpack was missing. She would have tried to find it in the woods, probably with very little luck, but the nice male nurse checking her vitals mentioned the dreamy, mysterious man who left her at the reception desk. He crooned on about the man's description the nurses gossiped about. It had to be Quint. She came back to his barn and found her bag.

"How am I supposed to keep you hidden? I have a job, and I don't live on this ranch alone. That doesn't include the guests. It's summer. We're booked solid through Labor Day."

"It's just a few days. I need some time to gather the evidence and to figure out my father's password. Other than a ride or two, you won't have to do anything else."

"If someone finds out you're with me, they're going to think I kidnapped you or worse, that I'm trying to help you put an end to Gray. I don't need that kind of trouble. I'll drive you someplace now, but after that, you're on your own."

"You've already lied for me. I didn't mean for you to get involved, but you are now. If the sheriff finds out I was here, he's going to make sure something bad happens to you. He's in on this with Tucker. An hour after I told the sheriff what I knew, Tucker and his men drove onto my property. They weren't coming for coffee."

He clasped his hands behind his head, stared at the ceiling, and let out a long breath. "Just for a couple of days?"

Hope blew a bubble in her chest. "I need to prove Dark Matter is full of steroids by the Montana Five Star. If he races, there won't be anything I can do. By the time another race comes up, Tucker will make sure no one ever listens to another word I say or I'll be dead. I'm halfway there now."

"What's your plan to prove all of this?" He leaned against the wall and glanced out the door.

"I have to find my father's journal where he kept track of all the medications he gave the horses. I'm hoping it's on his computer." She tapped the backpack.

Her father had always kept meticulous notes of his practice. She used to love watching him when she was little as he entered all the horses' names, medicines, and amounts into columns by hand with a black pen. He only used black pens.

When she found out he'd been taking money from Tucker to administer performance enhancing drugs to the race horses, everything she knew about her father changed. He wasn't the man she thought he was. He had always spoke of integrity and honor, only to find out that had been a lie. Everything about their lives had been a lie. They were broke, but he never told them. He had acted as if they were better than others. They came from the right neighborhood, knew the right people, played golf at the right club. He had been one of the ones to tell her Quint wasn't good enough for her. She had believed him.

"You only need his journals?" Quint's voice dragged her back into the shed that smelled of gasoline and dust.

"I also need a urine sample from Dark Matter, but I have to get that within twenty-four hours of the race." She would also need someone at the lab to test the sample, but she had no idea how she would get that to happen. Someone there could be in on Tucker's scheme. She didn't know who to trust. If she went to a lab outside of the county or state, she wouldn't have the test results back in time, and she'd only raise suspicions.

"You're going to have to break into his barn."

"Yes." She swallowed the fear in her throat. "It's the only way."

"What do I get out of this except a bag full of trouble and possibly face returning to jail? If I get caught helping you, Gray will make up an excuse to have me arrested. I'm not going back to jail for anyone."

"I'll give you money." She didn't have money since her practice was just about non-existent at this point.

Tucker was counting on her money troubles to persuade her to inject his horses with steroids. She'd rather go homeless than do what he wanted, and the fact her father had been doing it only made her sick.

"I don't want your money."

Her shoulders sagged. She was out of ideas to get this man to help her. If she was going to be honest, having someone like Quint beside her took some of the fear away. She didn't really know how to fight Tucker Gray. She certainly didn't want to sneak onto the racetrack full of people taking care of horses, the jockeys, and the owners by herself. Quint would know how to find his way in without getting caught. He had more than the bad boy reputation. He'd been doing things like breaking and entering since high school. All small stuff. Back then, he was just sexy in that unattainable way.

"I'm sorry I bothered you. I'll go now and leave you out of this. The only thing I ask is if you could not tell anyone you saw me here." She inched past him toward the door.

He gripped her arm and tugged her closer to him. He smelled woodsy with a hint of sweet spice. A shiver ran over her skin. "Don't go out there. My men will be taking care of the animals, and someone will see you. You'll stay here until I say it's safe to come out."

"You're going to help me?"

"I want something in return for my risk, but I don't want your money."

She tried to still her heart and meet his fierce gaze. "I won't sleep with you, if that's what you're getting at.

I'll take my chances with Tucker Gray before I agree to that."

He dropped her arm as if she burned his hand. She stumbled. "What kind of a man do you think I am?"

"I don't know." She would have been glad to take him into her bed if the circumstances were different. What was a man with a wild streak the size of the Continental Divide like during sex? But she couldn't trade her body for his help. It would be easier to inject the horses. She wanted to make love to a man when that's what it was.

"I'm not a man who asks for sex for favors, lady. I won't deny most of the rumors you've heard about me are true, but some of us cons have an honor code. When a woman comes into my bed, it's because that's exactly where she wants to be of her own free will." The fierceness in his eyes turned off like a light.

"I'm sorry. Of course, you wouldn't ask for that kind of payment."

"Stay put until I come back no matter how late it gets. If you have to pee, there's a bucket in the corner. If you take a step outside this shed, you're on your own." He turned on his heel and shut her in the shed.

Tears pricked her eyes, but she fought to keep them from coming. She tried the door. It moved under her touch. The choice to stay or go was hers. She'd go. She didn't need Quint Porter. All she had to do was get off the Weston Ranch and hide out somewhere else until she cracked the password and obtained Dark Matter's sample. Her hand hovered by the door latch.

Male voices drifted through the wood door. Someone was laughing. They were right outside the shed. She held her breath until the sounds were gone.

She returned to her hiding spot behind the ladders.

And waited.

CHAPTER 4

QUINT HURRIED TO THE SHED. He had meant to get back to Cheyenne hours ago, but every time he thought he could break away, another fire needed putting out. She might even be gone by now, which should be a good thing, but if he was going to be honest, he didn't want her trying to hide from Gray by herself. That man would eat her alive. Quint had no idea how to protect her, but he was tied to her now with his lie and keeping her in his shed. He groaned. That was a stupid idea, but he hadn't known what else to suggest.

The disgust on her face at the prospect of sleeping with him haunted him all day. It was as if she'd poked a hole in his chest. She was out of his league, but that didn't make the pain any less. They'd spent time together over the years. Nothing special. She'd come check on the horses. They'd see each other in town. There had been that date once in high school. He had considered asking her for coffee once or twice, but always thought better of it. People would give her a hard time for being with him. He didn't want that for her. Still, lying beside him wasn't the equivalent to lying with a snake. Or was it?

He pushed open the door. "Cheyenne?" Shadows spilled from the corners of the shed. He gave his eyes a minute to adjust to the inside.

She peeked around the ladder. Worry let go of the grip on his chest. "I'm sorry for taking so–"

"It's about damn time." She pushed out from behind the ladder. "My butt fell asleep. My legs are cramped, and I'm starving. I need to pee, which I wasn't going to do in that bucket."

He bit down on his cheek to keep from laughing. The fire in her voice warmed his insides. She had pinned up her long hair, which gave him a view of her slender neck and her collar bone that begged to be kissed. He tried not to stare.

"Are you just going to stand there with your mouth hanging open, or do you have a plan to get me out of this shed? I only have a few days to prove Tucker is a criminal, or my life as I know it will end permanently."

"Hey, I'm the one doing you a favor. You want to dial back that bark a little? I've been busy all day."

Her shoulders sagged, and she let out a long breath. "Fine. I'm sorry." She gave her head a small shake and squared her shoulders. The smile she painted on her face was all teeth. "Quint, my good friend, have you had an opportunity during your busy day to arrange a plan while I sat in this hot, smelly shed sweating my ass off and worrying that someone other than you would find out I'm here and put a bullet in my head?"

"That doesn't sound like dialing it back." His mouth wanted to curl up in response to her ornery mood, but he tried to keep a straight face. He could want a spitfire woman like the doctor wrapped in his sheets for a very long time. And that was plain foolish.

"I'll do better next time. What's the plan?"

"I arranged for us to spend the night in a cabin in Winter. We'll be safe there for however long you need."

"What do you mean 'you arranged'? You didn't tell Ty Weston about this, did you?"

He held up a hand to stop the runaway emotions brewing in her eyes. "Ty doesn't know a thing except I need a few days off. I spoke with Hank Patterson. He gave us the cabin. It belongs to one of his men. It's safe."

He hadn't known what else to do except call Hank. Cheyenne couldn't stay with him in his cabin here. Too many people could come by at any time. Even the sheriff could make an unexpected visit with the need to use his handcuffs. Quint needed help, and Hank was the only person who could be trusted. Hank had jumped at the chance to assist.

He was indebted to Hank Patterson now because of this beautiful and intriguing woman standing in the damn shed. Every minute with Cheyenne tangled him up like a hogtied pig.

"I sent my men into town for dinner. We can leave now and get to the cabin by nightfall. Jax Montero will meet us there and try to unlock your computer."

She narrowed her eyes. "Why is Hank willing to help me?"

He wanted to reassure her in some way that Hank would not turn on her. She had to know who Hank was and what he did. The Brotherhood Protectors weren't exactly a secret.

"Because you're in trouble and he protects people."

"I don't think I can afford to pay him."

"I'll take care of the payment." Payment was going to be his employment in the Brotherhood. Hank would never take no for an answer now, no matter how much he didn't want to be a full-time bodyguard.

"What payment is that going to be?"

"You can clean my stalls." He motioned for her to join him by the door. He grabbed her elbow and hurried to his truck parked nearby.

The sun was on its way out of the sky, and he was grateful for the cover of darkness to shield them on their way to the cabin.

She slid into the truck and he ran around the front to join her. She smelled of flowers and grass, and something faintly like tobacco. His heart picked up speed. He could not have this woman. She belonged to another world. One that would never invite him in. He checked the rearview mirror. Not because he thought anyone was following them, but because he might never return to the only place he ever called home and wanted one more look.

"When all of this is over, I'll find a way to pay Hank and you." She placed the backpack at her feet. Dark circles outlined her eyes. Her mouth was etched with pain and exhaustion.

He wanted to rest her head against his shoulder. This woman had stolen his horse and now his quiet, peaceful life.

"You can sleep if you want. I'll wake you when we get there." He turned right at the end of the road.

She closed her eyes and leaned her head back. "You're very nice."

"That surprises you." It wasn't a question.

"Maybe a little. I thought you might want to kill me for stealing your horse. I know how protective you are of all the animals on the ranch."

"I was pissed off at first." But when he saw her hurt, the anger had drained away.

She shifted in the seat and covered a yawn. "I like that you don't hide who you are. Everyone knows where they stand with you."

That comment surprised him.

"Can I ask you something?" She kept her eyes closed.

"Sure." He turned the truck off the highway and onto the side road.

"Is it a coincidence that every time you got in a fight, it was to protect a woman?"

His breath hitched. "No."

"I didn't think so. I am going to try and sleep. My head still hurts from the accident, and I was up all night." Her words slowed to a trot.

He opened his mouth to say something, then clamped it shut. She had seen a part of him he didn't think anyone else ever noticed and that left him without anything to say.

"Quint?" Her voice was a whisper.

"Yes?"

"In case I forget to say it, thank you." With her eyes still closed, she placed a hand on his thigh.

Her warm touch against his leg tore his attention from the road. The truck swerved to where the asphalt met the dirt. He righted the vehicle and tried to slow his heart. She hadn't moved. Her breath was deep and relaxed. The crease between her brow had smoothed out.

He gripped her hand to remove it from his leg, but brought it to his lips. Her soft skin only managed to light something inside him he thought was gone. He was headed for something dangerous, and it had nothing to do with Tucker Gray.

He held Cheyenne's hand for a second longer before putting both of his hands on the wheel.

Keep her hidden for a few days. After that, he'd have to move on. Far away from Montana. And far away from the beautiful woman with the power to undo him.

CHAPTER 5

"WE'RE HERE," Quint said.

His voice pulled her from the last dregs of sleep. Cheyenne's head throbbed, and her neck ached from the angle she slept at. "How long have I been out?"

"Two hours." He pushed out of the truck.

The sun had set while she was sleeping. Sparks of stars dotted the ink sky. The tops of trees brushed back and forth in the breeze like a horse's tail. One light on the porch of a log cabin welcomed them in. Darkness cloaked the house on all sides. She turned to glance out the back window and was met with nothing but more black. There wasn't anyone or anything around them.

Quint had arranged this for her. A smile tugged at her lips, but she forced it down. *Don't get too excited.* He might be nice, but she shouldn't trust him completely. Not yet, anyway. She had roped him into her mess, and if he decided at any minute, he had enough of her problems he would throw her to the lions. She needed to keep focused and not let sentimentality or hormones cloud her judgement.

Still, the idea that Quint took her safety into account and agreed to help her warmed her from the core out. He let his softer side slip out from his tough exterior. She wanted to see more of it the way she wanted to see him without a shirt on.

He banged on the truck door. She jumped. "You coming or are you going to sit there all night?"

He marched away but held the front door of the cabin open for her.

"Thanks." She slipped past him and tried to ignore that woodsy scent he wore so well.

The cabin was one big room with the living area up front and the kitchen in the back. The walls were paneled with knotted wood. Leather sofas offered a place to cuddle up and watch the fire. The granite counter and stainless-steel appliances indicated the space had been renovated recently.

"There are two bedrooms and a bathroom in the back. Do you want me to light the fire? It's a lot cooler at the top of the mountain than at home." Quint squatted down at the wood burning stove.

She was awarded with a view of his muscular back, wide shoulders, and thin waist. Working on a ranch agreed with him. Well, his results from working on a ranch agreed with her.

"I'm fine. When will Jax come to help us?"

She needed to keep her thoughts on something practical and not the fine definition of his muscles or the idea of cuddling up against him beside a fire. Everything that happened in the past several hours must be the explanation for her overactive libido. She hadn't wanted a man in a long time. Too much trouble, but here she was curious about Quint's naked body.

"He should be here soon. There's food if you're hungry." He pointed to the cabinets.

"I think I'll go find that bathroom." She took her backpack and closed the door to the small bathroom.

She splashed cold water on her face to calm her nerves. This was crazy. She had officially taken on Tucker Gray. Maybe she'd be alright. Maybe by the end of the week she could have her life back. But only if they cracked the password.

Tucker hadn't wasted any time after her father's death to demand she inject the horses. Foolishly, she had no idea what her father was up to.

She assumed her father's notes were on the computer, but had searched everywhere in the office for his old notebooks to no avail. If they weren't on the computer, she didn't know where else to look. And if she was wrong about her father documenting the illegal medications given to the horses, the urine test might not be enough.

She pressed her cool hands to her burning cheeks. Her head continued to pound. She needed more rest, but not tonight. When this was all over, she'd rest then.

"Cheyenne, um, you might want to hurry up. Jax is here." Quint knocked on the door.

She pulled it open to find him with his hands in his back pockets and a red flush on his cheeks. "Does knocking on a bathroom door when a lady is taking a pee embarrass you?"

"No." The blush deepened against his pale skin.

"You've seen cows do worse, trust me." Ruffling Quint's feathers gave her a rush. He always seemed unshakeable. Funny how a bathroom break could set him off balance.

"Hi, I'm Jax Montero." He raised his hand in a wave.

He wore a wedding ring and a large smile. Jax was handsome with his black hair and tan skin. She preferred Quint's solid build and scruffy jaw. She stole a glance at her new bodyguard, and a shiver ran over her. He would never want her. She was just lonely. Quint was always off limits, and that made him more exciting.

"Thanks for coming. Do you think you can figure out the password?" She pulled the computer out of the backpack.

Jax took a seat at the high-top kitchen table and pulled the computer close to him. "I'll do my best. My partner is the one who can handle any computer, but he's helping out on another assignment. We need you, Quint."

"I keep telling you no."

She looked between the two men. Jax still smiled.

Quint grimaced. Quint didn't want to work with the Brotherhood, but Hank must really want him.

They went through the obvious choices for passwords. Jax had some clever questions that made her think of other possibilities her father might have used, but nothing worked. She wanted to call Koda for ideas, but her brother had to think she was missing. He would only get dragged into this mess, and she couldn't allow that to happen. She missed him. Ever since this situation with Tucker Gray began, she'd been avoiding him. He didn't understand why, but she had tried to keep him off Tucker's radar as much as possible. Koda never worked with her and her father. He led a simple life two counties away. She envied him that.

Jax unplugged a small black box from her computer. "I'm sorry. I can't figure it out. Can I take this and let Lincoln play around with it? He'll be back tomorrow."

She sucked in a breath. "That's my only proof."

"I understand your concern, but you can trust me. I get paid pretty well to guard people and their belongings. Nothing will happen to your computer on my watch." Jax smiled again. It was a reassuring smile, and he worked for Hank, but she hesitated.

If that computer went missing, even by accident, she would never know what was on it. If she couldn't get the urine sample, she'd have to stay hidden for her entire life. Tucker would look for her. She had told on him. He would never let that go.

"Cheyenne, give it to him." Quint tilted his head in Jax's direction.

She tried to read his expression, but he kept his face neutral. Her instincts said no. She should keep the computer, but Quint gave her a small nod.

"Go on, now," he said.

"Okay." She let out a long breath.

"I'll come back tomorrow night either way." Jax shook Quint's hand then hers and left.

The door shut with a swoosh and separated her from possibly her only chance to survive this. "How could I let him take that?" She ran for the door.

Quint grabbed her by the waist and spun her around. He plopped her down facing him and blocked her path to the one thing she wanted.

"Stay put. That man knows what he's doing." He crossed his arms over his chest.

"Oh, yeah? Then why don't you work for them?"

"What?"

"Why should I trust him? Or you?" Logic slipped from her fingers. She needed her computer back where it would be safe. She could figure out the password on her own. She'd always had to rely on herself for everything. Now shouldn't be any different. She tried to dodge him, but he anticipated her move and cut her off.

"I'm about all you've got right now. Whether you like it or not, we're stuck together until this is over. And for the record, I don't like you much either."

She stumbled back as if he'd swung at her. "Me? I've never done anything to you."

"No? You steal my horse and get me caught up in your trouble. And what have I done since that minute you ran into the woods? I have helped you, and you stand there and tell me you don't trust me. I'm the only person you can trust, lady. How about that? You have to trust a killer." Anger burned in his eyes.

"Why'd you kill that man? Why didn't you stop?"

"Why did you hurt those animals?"

"I never did those things people are saying. Tucker made it all up. Everyone in the county believes him or is in his pocket. I can't fight that. He figured if he ruined me, I would do what he said, but I won't. It would have been easier to inject the horses, but I would rather die than be indebted to him or to ever hurt an innocent animal." Her hands shook. Tears burned her throat. She blinked several times and took a deep breath. She would not cry in front of this man.

"I know what it's like to have people judge you without knowing the whole story. I see the way you take care of the animals on the ranch. You would never hurt them. You can trust me. Not every rumor about me is true either." He dropped down on the couch as if the fight went out of him.

She sat in the corner of the couch, keeping space between them, but his sensibility took her breath away. "I'm sorry I said I didn't trust you. I panicked when Jax took my computer, and I shouldn't have asked you about that fight. It's none of my business." If this were any other time, she might fall for this guy if he was offering. Which he wasn't.

"I don't talk about that night." He rubbed his hands on his thighs and stood. "It's late. You should get some sleep. I think you'll be more comfortable in the room with the bigger bed. I'll sleep out here on the couch."

"Why don't you take the other room?"

He laughed. His eyes lit up for the first time. "You haven't seen those bunk beds. They weren't made for a man my size." He winked.

Her heart wobbled. "Okay, then. I wish we had stopped for some toiletries." Sweaters coated her teeth. She needed a shower and a fresh set of clothes.

"Everything you need will be in the bathroom. There's a washer and dryer too. We can wash our clothes. There's also a general store not too far away. I can go pick up what you need, but you have to stay here. Hank's orders."

"This really is a safe house. Why don't you want to work for them?" She wanted to know what drove him to be who he was.

"Not worth talking about. Holler when you're done in the bathroom." He ended the conversation by giving her his back.

"Is it the pay?" She wouldn't let him get away that easily.

"You're one stubborn woman." He didn't turn around.

"My American Indian grandfather said I got that from him. I guess that's why I'm in the trouble I'm in. If it isn't the money, then what's stopping you?"

He finally met her gaze. "My life is just fine the way it is. No complications. I know how to do my job. Another career isn't for me."

"In case you didn't realize, you're doing a pretty good job at keeping me safe. You're better at this bodyguard thing than you give yourself credit for. Good night, Quint. I'll let you know when you can brush your teeth."

She left him alone and got ready for bed. She turned off the lamp and stared out the window. The moon offered enough light to see into the trees. She hoped no one found them. It would be nice to stay here and forget about the rest of the world. She could forget about Tucker Gray while she was up here in this mountain. But someone had to take care of those horses, and it had to be her.

Quint moved around right outside her door. She meant what she said about him keeping her safe. If someone had asked her two days ago if she would rely on Quint Porter to protect her, she would have laughed.

But tonight...tonight her heart and head knew better.

CHAPTER 6

QUINT THREW off the blanket and went outside. He couldn't sleep with Cheyenne only feet away from him. Her intoxicating smell was everywhere, and the image of her bright-blue eyes daring him to believe he might be something played in his mind like a song. Her combination of light eyes and dark skin made her striking. He wanted to keep staring at her, but he didn't want to seem like some freak either. It was easier to turn his back on her.

The brisk night mountain air did nothing to cool his heated skin. Nothing was going to cool him off except to taste Cheyenne's full lips, and to have the weight of her pressed against him with nothing between them. He ran a hand over his face. He had lost his fucking mind in the past forty-eight hours. He wanted to go back to the moment before she changed his life forever. And that was never going to happen.

He could last a few more days with her. He had spent two years in jail. Babysitting her should be easy, but it was getting harder every minute. He wanted to hurt Gray. If he got his hands around that man's neck, he would snap it in half. Gray hurt animals, and he hurt Cheyenne. Quint would be justified, but he learned his lesson. No more vigilantism. What he was doing here with Cheyenne was as close to that as he would ever dare to get. If he hadn't had some help from Hank, he wouldn't even have done this much.

He also wanted to keep Cheyenne safe and not because he had Hank's help. Because she had put her trust in him when she didn't have any reason to. Something dangerous stirred in his chest. He needed that emotion to simmer down.

"Quint?"

He spun around. "Shit. You need to stop sneaking up on me."

She dipped her head, and her black hair fell over her face. He resisted the urge to tuck it behind her ear.

"Sorry." She chewed on her bottom lip. If she continued to do that, he would lose his resolve and kiss her.

She wore his flannel shirt still, but nothing on her legs. Her feet were bare too. He took a step back.

"You can't sleep?" He couldn't think of much else to say.

"I woke up, and for a second I couldn't remember where I was. Then I kept thinking about the problems I created. Sleep isn't in the plan for a few hours. You couldn't sleep either?"

"Too hot in there." Not a total lie. "You want to sit?" Two rocking chairs faced the woods and the long drive back to the road.

She tucked her legs under herself. He sat beside her and kept his gaze straight ahead.

"I want to go back to my father's house tomorrow. I didn't check his attic for his notebooks. Will you drive me?"

"Let's wait for Jax to come back with your computer first. No point in risking someone seeing you if what you need is on that computer." He wanted her to stay put and follow the directions given to her, but that stubborn streak would drive her to do what she shouldn't.

"If he's not back by suppertime, I'm going if I have to take your truck."

"That would not be wise." He peered at her from the corner of his eye.

"You can't stop me." She tilted her pretty chin up.

"I can, and I will. I didn't want to be your body-guard, but now I am. You will stay here until Jax calls or comes back no matter what time that is." He would tie her up if he had to. It would be for her own good.

"The race is in a few days. I have to get to Dark Matter before that."

"I know when the race is."

"I'm going to those stables even if Jax hasn't

returned. I want you to be clear about that. I won't hold you responsible if anything happens to me after you told me to stay. I'll sign whatever you want. I'll call Hank. But I need that urine sample twenty-four hours before the race." She stood and paced before him.

The edges of the flannel shirt fluttered as she went by and revealed more of her leg. He pushed out of the rocker and grabbed her by the arms. He stood close enough to force her to look up at him. Her wide-eyed stare and her sweet smell made the world tilt. He gripped her tighter to keep from losing his balance.

"You will do exactly as you're told. Do you hear me? I can't keep you safe if you go running around like some lunatic. Do you want to end up dead? Because you will."

The color drained from her face. "You're hurting me."

He dropped his grip as if her skin were hot. She backed away from him.

"I'm sorry. I didn't mean to —"

"Shut up. I —"

"Cheyenne, I swear I didn't mean to hurt you." Fear and desire had him acting out of control. How was he going to explain that to her? She wouldn't believe he was afraid something bad would happen to her. She might believe he wanted her, but in a violent way. Not the way he would ever touch her. He would love her the way she deserved it. Slow. Sweet. Steady. And it wouldn't be for one night. Cheyenne was worth more than one night.

"Why did you kill that man?" She wrapped her arms around her middle.

He would rather have her yell at him. Punch him even, but to stare at him with an expectation of the truth sucked the air from his lungs. He didn't talk about that night. "Please accept my apology. I shouldn't have grabbed you without your permission."

"I'll accept your apology when you tell me why you killed that man." She leaned against the porch column.

He stepped off the porch and put his back to her again. "Why do you want to hear that story?" There was no good reason to share that memory. It was his and his alone.

"I think you cared about someone, and they were getting hurt. You wanted to stop that. The fire in your eyes when I said I was going without you wasn't anger or violence. It was more than that."

"How do you know that by looking at me?" He continued to keep his back turned because he didn't trust himself with her. He would take her in his arms if he stared into her eyes now.

Her hand gripped his arm, and her heat rolled into him. "I'm a large animal vet, dummy. Horses tell us a lot through their eyes if you're paying attention."

He couldn't help it. The humor in her voice had him looking at her. "I'm no good."

Her gaze bore into his, and she smiled at him. "Tell me what happened."

The pain in his chest eased a little. "It was a long time ago." But the memory was as real as this moment standing with Cheyenne. "I was at the bar. Probably had too many drinks. Sarah was there with her new man. I knew I shouldn't be angry about her moving on from me, but I was anyway." He had already said too much to this woman. When he said the rest, she would look at him different. He liked the glint in her eye now. What would replace that look when she heard the end of the story?

"You two were together a long time."

She knew him well enough to fill in some of the blank spaces he wanted to leave open. He and Sarah had been together five years when she told him she didn't love him. Probably never had. She had found a real man. A man she could be proud to show-off. Not like him with his reputation for fighting.

"Were you ever in love?" He had to know what kind of a man could swipe her heart.

She leaned her head against his shoulder. "At my age, I should've been, but I let work get in the way of everything. When my dad got sick a few years ago, and I came home to help out, I never bothered to get involved. There wasn't enough space for love in my life."

A man would be lucky to love Cheyenne Locklear with her mocha skin and light eyes. She had made something of herself and stuck to her principles if running from Gray said anything.

"Please finish telling me your story."

"Why do you want to know so bad?"

"Because it's a part of who you are, and I want to get to know you better."

"There are better ways to get to know me."

She laughed and the pain in his chest eased a little more. He laced his arm around her shoulders to pull her closer and ward off some of the chill. "On lonely nights, after Sarah left me, I could hear her laughing at me. The way she ended things between us pissed me off. I was mad all the time. Mad at her. Mad at the world. But none of that mattered when I saw him slap her across the face. Her head snapped back, and she fell over the pool table. The place went quiet. No one moved. I knocked over the bar stool and jumped the half wall. I started swinging."

"They arrested you and pressed charges because you had been in the army and had skills. You didn't stand a chance."

"I hit him because I was drunk and mad." He waited for her to move away from him, but she stayed put. "They arrested me because I killed him." The words cut his tongue on the way out of his mouth. He hadn't meant to kill him, but that didn't matter. The result was the same.

"You didn't mean to kill him." Her words echoed his thoughts, but floated away in the wind. He wanted to chase them down and press them against the hole in his heart.

"You don't know what I meant." He wouldn't allow himself to believe she might understand. No one understood what had happened.

She looked up at him. "You saw what your father did to your mother."

"Damn it, Cheyenne, don't bring that up." Heat burned his neck and face. She knew. Everyone in their small town suspected the secret bursting in the Porter house. He didn't want to relive it with her pressed against his side smelling sweet and stealing his breath. When he thought about his life growing up, shame stripped away his ability to be a man.

She faced him and pressed a hand to his chest. Her touch set him on fire. "You won't allow a woman to be hurt because your mother was. There's no crime in that. Your father was a bad man. You aren't."

He took her hand in his. "I am. I work on the ranch because I can keep to myself. I take my anger out on my job. I work hard every day until I break. Then I go back to my house and drop from exhaustion. You came along and shook that all up. You're scared, and I'm here. You don't know me."

"I know you are the only man capable of keeping me safe from Tucker Gray. When I ran into your barn to take Moon, I had hoped you'd follow me even though I was scared you'd be furious enough to strangle me."

"I would never lay a hand on you." He had been ready to kill whoever took his horse. His anger still had control of him, but he would never hurt her. He hoped she understood that.

"Your horse was going to be my ticket free. If you followed me, I planned to beg you to help me get to the county sheriff."

"What if I hadn't followed you?"

"Then I was going to the county myself and return Moon later. You're here because I wanted it that way." She looked up at him through her long lashes.

Something like hope snaked up his throat, but he wouldn't let it take hold. "What are you saying?"

He had wanted her once, a long time ago, but they had been young, and she had been under her father's thumb. He forbade Cheyenne to see him again, and she had listened. He understood even though his chest burned as if he'd been branded.

And he had been branded by his father's drunken, evil streak. His father had lied and stolen from every man he worked for. He drank and beat his wife. When Quint got old enough and strong enough, he fought back. He'd broken his father's nose and pulled a knife on him. His father left the next day.

"I'm saying, kiss me, Quint, before I do something to embarrass myself further."

He cupped her face and pulled her to him. Her lips were soft like the skin on her hands. Heat poured over him as she wrapped her arms around his neck and kissed him back.

He wanted more. He teased her lips apart with his tongue. When she surrendered to him and opened her mouth, his head spun. He could have been standing in the stars at that moment.

Her hands went under his shirt and up his back. He shivered, and she did it again. He cupped her bottom and pressed her to him. She was driving him crazy. He wanted her to know how much.

She wrapped one leg around his hip and grinded against him. The friction through his jeans made him want to tear his flannel shirt off her. "Let's go inside," he said.

She kept her leg where it was and smiled up at him. "Did you want to do something else? I'm kind of having a good time right here."

He scooped her up and flipped her over his shoulder in one swift move. Her shirt bunched up under his arm revealing her butt. She wore black, lacy panties that covered only the top half. His dick pressed hard against his zipper.

"Quint." She laughed and swatted his backside.

He strode into the house and kicked the door shut not to let go of her. He took her to the bedroom and eased her down.

"You have a nice laugh." He smoothed her silky hair away from her face the way he wanted to earlier.

"Thank you. Now, where were we?" She reached for his shirt, but he grabbed her hands.

"You don't have to do this. You don't owe me anything."

"I don't understand. You don't like me?" She narrowed her eyes.

"Shit, that's not it. I'm trying to save you from regretting this decision in the morning."

"You're killing the mood." She unbuttoned the flannel and let it drop to the floor.

He was all done talking.

CHEYENNE'S LEGS quivered as she stood before Quint in nothing but her underwear. She had never been so impulsive as she had been these past few days. Running for her life flipped a switch she didn't even know she had.

Quint's dark gaze burned into hers. He stepped closer and tangled his fingers in her hair. She couldn't wait and kissed him first. He tasted like running water. She wanted more and took the kiss deeper. His moan turned up her desire.

Her hands sought his warm skin. She ran her fingers up his back again. He seemed to like it before. His muscles flexed under her touch, and the breath left her lungs. He was strong from working the ranch. She lifted his shirt over his head and stepped back to see him better.

"You are gorgeous," she said.

He gave her a knowing smile and reached for her.

She pressed against his chest and kissed his collarbone. Her fingers explored the soft hair on his chest. He gripped her waist with one hand and tilted her chin up with the other.

"Wait," she said.

She brought her lips back to his shoulder. She needed to taste all of him. She didn't want to miss one part. She left a wet trail of kisses down his front. Her lips followed the trail her fingers started. She let her tongue linger around his nipples. He groaned again, and the power of her effect on him sent her head spinning. No one could control Quint and here she was taming him.

She continued to follow the line of his chest hair until she neared his navel. Her fingers fought with the button of his jeans.

"Hang on." He gripped her shoulders and pulled her up. "Not so fast."

He turned the bed down and held the sheet up for her to slide under. The cotton was cool against her already heated skin. He stripped off the rest of his clothes and joined her.

He brought her to him so they could lay facing each other. His erection pressed against her belly. She wanted to feel him in her hand, but she waited because he had asked her to.

He tucked her hair behind her ear and kissed her again. His hands traveled over her body as if he was studying her. He lingered at one breast by taking the nub between his fingers and rubbing until it was hard. She arched her back to get more.

"Do you like that?" He moved his lips to her other nipple. If she could, she would fly away on the desire inside her.

His teeth nipped at her sensitive skin while his hand continued to caress her other breast. She ran her hands over his body, going lower.

He grabbed her hand. "Not yet."

"You're driving me a little crazy here."

"We're not in any rush."

His quiet, stoic side always intrigued her. He was a puzzle she wanted to figure out. What would be the thing to get him to open up and let someone in?

"Quint, do you remember that night when we went to dinner?"

He stopped kissing her side and looked up at her. "I do. Why?"

"I'm sorry for what happened."

"Nothing to worry about. It was a long time ago, but if you're having regrets about us tonight, you need to tell me now. I'll climb right out of this bed and put my pants back on."

"I want you to know I've always liked you. This isn't

just about tonight. I wasn't brave enough to do anything about it until now."

He rubbed the ends of her hair between his fingers. "Are you done talking, because I want to show you how I feel about you."

Desire rippled against her skin. She pulled him up so she could kiss him again. His lips on her body were ecstasy, but she needed to taste him. She had never wanted a man as much as she wanted him. His strength turned her on and her world on its head. She had been a fool to listen to her father all those years ago. Quint's family didn't matter nor did what side of the tracks he lived on. She wasn't anything special and the worst part was neither was her father. He'd been a hypocrite judging Quint. She didn't even care about his time in jail because he wasn't a criminal. He was a man with a heart who shut it off to the world.

His fingers slid from her thigh to between her legs. Heat rolled off her in waves. He hadn't even touched her most sensitive spot, and all she wanted was to feel him inside her.

"Please touch me." She dragged her hand over his flat stomach and gripped him.

He growled and nipped at her earlobe. Her hand wrapped around him. Touching him only made her hot enough to burn every forest in Montana to the ground.

His finger slid inside her and stroked. She arched her hips, needing him. It still wasn't enough. She moved his hand away and pushed him on his back.

She straddled him and raked her fingers over his chest. He moved beneath her. The bristle of his pubic hair excited her more. She took him in her hand and lined up their bodies. Without another thought, she slid him inside her.

She forgot everything else except the way their bodies moved together. She leaned back and rocked until the burning need exploded. She shook from head to toe and called out his name. With a final shudder, she dropped her head to his chest and gulped in air.

He gripped her hips and turned her so she was on her back. He held her gaze and moved inside her with a fierce determination until he met her on the other side of the sweet pleasure.

CHAPTER 7

CHEYENNE WOKE UP ALONE. She covered her face with the pillow. It smelled of his woodsy scent. She tossed it aside. Seducing Quint might have been a mistake, but she couldn't help herself. Everything about him was sexy. She couldn't even run away and die from embarrassment in peace because she still needed him to get her to the stables. How was she going to look the man in the eye after what they shared last night? She had never been that forward with a man, but she had been at ease with him. He made her feel safe.

If he couldn't wake up beside her, he must be regretting what they did. What did she think he was going to do? Fall in love with her? He was helping her because he felt as if he had no choice. A position she put him in him, she should remember. She covered her face again. *Was that pity sex?*

"Good morning, darlin'." Quint's voice made her sit up.

She gathered the sheets around her. He eased into the bedroom wearing only his jeans with the button undone, revealing the top of his black boxer-briefs and the soft hair that led to his very capable man parts. His sculpted chest took her breath away. He carried two mugs and handed her one.

"Hi." It was all she could manage for the moment. Maybe he didn't regret what happened after all. She sipped the hot, black coffee, but eyed him over the top of the mug.

He sat beside her and placed a soft kiss on her lips. "I don't sleep much. I hope you didn't mind waking up alone."

"It's fine. I'm sure you were more comfortable on the couch." After they had made love, he had gathered her in his arms. For the first time in a very long time, she had felt secure knowing no one would come after her. She had fallen asleep in seconds.

When her situation was over, would they go back to waving to each other over the fence line? She could handle whatever happened between them. She liked him, and if he felt the same way, she'd gladly share her bed with him, but if he got what he wanted from her last night, she could live with that too. She didn't need him. She wanted him.

"Only the habit of waking for the ranch got me out

of this bed. I didn't want to disturb you, so I let you sleep. I can make you breakfast if you're hungry."

"You cook too?"

"I can handle eggs."

He could handle way more than that. A shiver ran over her body as she thought of the way he touched her. The last thing she wanted was eggs. She put the mug down on the table beside the bed, and let the sheet drop.

He smiled and placed his mug beside hers. He cupped her face and kissed her until her mind emptied of any thought except for thoughts of him. Her hands explored his chest, already knowing each angle, but he eased back.

"Darlin', nothing would give me greater pleasure than to climb back into bed with you. But Jax called this morning. He's on his way."

"Did he figure out how to get into the computer?" She jumped from the bed and started gathering up her clothes. This was her big chance. She'd have the proof she needed.

He dropped his gaze, and her heart stuttered.

"Quint, don't hide anything from me. What did he say?"

He looked at her with a clouded stare. "No luck."

"But did his partner check it? He said—"

His shaking head stopped the words in her throat. "They spoke on the phone. Lincoln talked him through the steps. Nothing. You'll have to keep thinking. I'm sorry."

"You need to take me to my father's house today. I'm going to take a shower." She turned away from him afraid she might cry and went into the bathroom.

"Cheyenne, Jax wants you to stay put," he called after her.

The sadness and the anger returned her to the bedroom. He needed to understand how important this was for her. She pointed a finger at him. "You listen to me, Quint Porter. I'm going to my daddy's house today with or without you. I need those notebooks, and if I can't get into his computer then I pray he kept a hard copy someplace. And tomorrow you're going to take me to the racetrack so I can steal a urine sample from a horse. Am I clear enough for you?"

He met her in the doorway and stood close enough she had to tilt her chin to meet his glare. She wasn't backing off.

"You telling me?" He stared down at her with that fierceness in his eyes.

"I am."

"Even though it's not how I want to keep you safe."

"I have to do this."

He pressed a kiss on her lips and kept his head bent to hers. "Last night changed things. I can't let anything happen to you. I'll kill someone if you get hurt."

She placed a hand on his cheek. His beard scratched her fingers, and the idea that she meant something to him stole her breath. "After tomorrow, when I prove Tucker Gray is hurting those horses, you can protect me your way. If you want."

"I want."

QUINT TOOK the computer from Jax and shook his hand. "Thanks."

Jax hitched a leg into his truck and closed the door. "We'll figure out that password. I just hope when we do, she finds what she's looking for."

He did too. "What if she can't prove Gray is injecting those horses?"

"Hank can get her someplace safe. She'd have to leave town. Maybe change her name." Jax kicked over the engine.

"Is her brother still looking for her?"

"The whole town is. Hank planted some evidence to keep the wheels spinning. No one will find her before that race. Looks like you're working for the Brotherhood, man. Welcome aboard." Jax laughed.

"This is a one-time thing. I want to help Cheyenne."

"Stop fighting it. You belong on our team."

"I'll pay Hank for his time and resources. I'm not joining." If Cheyenne went on the run, he'd go too unless she told him not to and that was still a possibility. She didn't need him and one night together didn't change that for her. She might've gotten what she wanted out of him.

"You know, when I left the force, I was pissed at the world. I'd been shot, my woman had left me, and I'd lost my baby. Hank came to the hospital to see me. He offered me a job. I threw the bed pan at him. I never believed I'd get a second chance at life. Hank often knows what we need when we don't." Jax shook his head. "Listen to me. I sound like some damn self-help book. I'll be in touch." He sped away down the driveway.

He didn't care what Jax said. They weren't the same. Getting a second chance might be too much to ask for a man like him. He took the computer inside and forced thoughts of a future out of his head.

Cheyenne met him in the living room. "Can we go now?"

"You don't want to at least wait until it's dark?" He couldn't talk her out of going, but he still tried.

"I can't sit around all day." She tied her hair up with a black rubber band.

He wanted to run his tongue over her neck, but she would slap him if he tried that now. She was determined to go on her mission, and she would not stand for him distracting her. "Let's go then."

She smiled up at him. "Thank you."

He held her chin between his fingers and memorized her face in case this ended with them going separate ways. "Don't make me regret this decision."

"You won't. I promise." She met his gaze with her spirited one.

Her strength made him want her all over again. She fought for something bigger than she was, and she wasn't afraid. He could fall in love with a small shove.

"I'll show you my appreciation tonight, cowboy." She stepped aside and marched out of the house.

"Yes, ma'am." And he followed her.

CHAPTER 8

SWEAT RAN into Cheyenne's eyes. She swiped it away with the back of her hand. The attic of her dad's house was hotter than the center of the earth and packed with crap from the past forty years. She couldn't find the notebooks. Tears burned her eyes, but she had no time for crying.

"Cheyenne, how much longer?" Quint popped up through the hole in the floor and climbed into the attic. He ducked under a beam and squatted down beside her. She resisted the urge to run her hand over his solid thigh.

"I just want to go through this filing cabinet behind these boxes." She tugged on the bottom drawer and shook the cabinet. Years of dust invaded her nose.

Papers and folders stuffed the drawer like a burrito. Her shoulders sagged. She'd have to go through every one. This was the last place to look. If the notebooks weren't in the filing cabinet, her father hadn't kept a copy anywhere.

Quint looked out the small window. "You're running out of daylight. Remember what I said."

"Don't turn on any lights." She rolled her eyes and held up the flashlight he gave her.

"Stop sassin' me. I'm trying to keep you safe."

"I know you are, but you need a little sass in your life." She blew him a kiss.

"I like my life boring and quiet. There's a lot of stuff up here." He moved around the attic looking inside boxes.

He loved his life on the ranch and wasn't about to give it up. Not that she would ask him to. She doubted she could make him happy. They both loved horses, but what else did they have in common? Quint wasn't a man to settle down with a wife and a family. She sighed. Her time to even have children was quickly passing her by. She would never have a family of her own.

"My parents bought the house when Koda was born. Dad was the first person in his family to own a home. He kept everything. I think it was because he grew up poor."

"Darlin', no disrespect to your dad, but I grew up poor, and I didn't save half this much stuff." Quint pulled a photograph out of a box. "You have your mother's eyes."

She took the picture from him. Her mother stood in

front of their old station wagon in her bell bottom jeans and striped, flowing shirt. She held a cigarette in one hand and gave her biggest smile to the camera. She had been young and full of promise that day. "I miss her every day."

He placed a kiss on her lips. "I know what you mean. I'll be downstairs keeping watch, but don't take too much longer."

"Thank you for keeping an eye out." She owed him so much.

"Glad to do it, but hurry up now. I want to get back to the cabin." He dropped out of sight.

She went back to her task. The sun set and left the attic drenched in long shadows. The heat never lessened, and her eyes hurt from straining to see by the small beam of the flashlight. Still no sign of the notebooks. She couldn't allow defeat to stop her. She could get the urine sample tomorrow. With that, she had a chance to disqualify the horse from running.

Disqualifying the horse was something, but it wasn't enough because Tucker would hunt her down for making him lose the race and a lot of money. She would have to find a way to hide for the rest of her life. Where would she go?

She opened the top drawer of the filing cabinet and wiped her sweaty hands on her pants. She gripped the flashlight in her teeth. The drawer was filled with old greeting cards and utility bills. She grabbed them and shoved them to the side. A stack of four marble notebooks stared up at her. The flashlight fell. She scrambled around on the floor for the light and held it over the drawer again. With a deep breath and shaking hands, she grabbed the notebooks.

Quint pounded up the steps. "Cheyenne, we have to go now."

She jumped. "Why?"

"Now. No time for talking." He waved his hand.

She ran and tripped over a box. The notebooks spilled. Her hands dragged along the plywood floor, and her skin split open. He gripped her under the arms and pulled her up.

"I need those books." She tore her arm free.

He gathered the books and tucked them under his arm. "Let's go."

They hurried through the house. He stopped her at the kitchen door and pushed her behind him.

"What's happening?" She kept her voice low.

"Someone pulled into the driveway. I think whoever it is went to the garage."

The backyard was five acres deep. The detached garage sat way in the back with its doors opened in a yawn. Her father kept lawn equipment in there.

"There's no way someone knows we're here. The house has sat empty for a year." She was sure no one followed them. Quint had taken back roads, drove in circles for an extra hour, and had her face backward almost the whole time looking out the window for signs of a car.

He stared at her now. "I saw movement and I heard gravel being kicked. That person making noise is looking for you. Jax said the whole town is on the lookout."

"What do we do?" Her heart picked up speed again.

They were trapped. She could barely see into the yard because the clouds covered any moonlight. Quint's truck was on the other side of the property behind the garage. He had parked in the thick tree line, and they walked over.

"We're going to make a run for it."

"I won't be able to keep up with you." He was a foot taller than her. His long legs would clear the space in no time.

"I won't leave you behind, darlin'." He kissed her lips. "I need you to trust me. Can you do that just this once?"

"I trust you completely." She hadn't thought that possible. Even though Quint could keep her safe, and that's why she stole his horse, until the other night, she wasn't totally sure if he was pushed into a corner what he would do.

"All right then. Stay as close as you can to me." He took her hand and opened the door.

Instead of running toward the tree line and the garage, he banked to the right. She wanted to ask what he was thinking. They would have to run a half-mile this way. But he'd asked her to trust him.

Her legs pumped to keep up with him, and her

lungs burned with each step, but he gripped her hand and dragged her along. As long as he didn't let go, she'd be okay.

He stopped short, and she collided into his back. He held her against him. "Who's there?" His voice demanded an answer.

"What's happening?" She whispered into his shirt.

"Hush." He muttered. "I know you're out there. Show your face." Quint stepped to the side and kept her behind him.

They needed to get to the trees for coverage. Out in the open, they were exposed. He must know that. She tugged on his shirt to get his attention.

He spun around and pushed her behind him. "I mean it now. You're going to have to get through me to get to the lady."

She strained to hear what he heard. Her heart pounded in her ears and blocked all other sounds. But he must not be sure where this person was if he kept turning in circles.

He took her hand again. A branch snapped somewhere in front of them. She froze. Quint's lips were near her ear.

"Go back to the house and stay there until I come for you. Don't say a word. Just go."

She shook her head. She would not leave him.

"I asked you to trust me. There's no time." He kissed her. "I'll be back." He shoved the notebooks at her and disappeared into the vast darkness.

Her legs carried her back to the house. She locked the door and rummaged through the drawers for some kind of weapon. She wanted to be with Quint and not hiding in the dark by herself. She shouldn't have let him go alone. He said to trust him, but he didn't have to do this by himself. This wasn't his fight, and yet he'd made it his.

She counted the seconds. If he didn't return soon, she'd go looking for him. It would only be a matter of time before whoever was out there would come inside the house if Quint couldn't stop them. She didn't want to think about what kind of torture Tucker Gray would inflict on her if Quint was hurt. Her fingers gripped a rolling pin.

A loud, booming sound ricocheted through the trees. She dropped the rolling pin and peered through the bottom of the window. A reddish light in the distance faded, and someone moved in the yard. She dropped back down and gulped in air. She had to be sure of what she saw before she made the decision to leave Quint behind. If she just saw the muzzle flash of a gun, he was dead.

She held her breath and looked again. The air escaped her lungs. She yanked open the door. "Quint."

She ran, but didn't get to him before he collapsed.

QUINT FOUGHT to open his eyes. His clothes were wet.

Someone was dragging him. A pain throbbed in his side. Cheyenne's sweet moonflower scent hovered over him.

"Darlin', stop." He gripped her arm and hoped she'd let go of him. Bumping over the wet, uneven ground didn't help the pain in his side.

She dropped down beside him. "We have to get you inside."

"Let me walk."

"You're all right? I saw you fall. I didn't know what happened." Her hands were all over him searching.

"Oh no." She froze above him.

"I've been shot."

"I can see that. Shit. Shit. Shit. Can you stand? No, don't get up. I'll carry you." She fought to get her arms under his.

He laughed, and it sent another dose of pain up his side and made him cough. "You can't carry me. It's just a flesh wound."

"Flesh wound? You were just unconscious. Stop being such a man."

"No more dragging me. I'll walk. Like a man."

She helped him stand and wrapped an arm around his waist. His head spun, and his stomach threatened to bring up its contents. They cleared the rest of the yard and made it back to the house. She settled him on the couch in the front room. He made her lock the doors and keep the lights off.

"I need more light to see the damage." She held the small flashlight over the gash in his side.

Blood ran into the waistband of his jeans. The edges of the wound were shredded as if someone had tried to cut him open with a jagged knife. He'd been in worse scrapes.

"The bullet looks like it went straight through. I don't have my medical bag, but I might have a few things in my backpack. I need to clean this."

"Do your best, but hurry. I might have sent that guy off running, but it doesn't mean he won't come back and with help. We need to get the hell out of here and back to the cabin."

"What happened?" She pressed a dish towel to his side.

He tucked her hair behind her ear. He could run his fingers through her hair all day. He wanted to ask her what she thought about living on the ranch with him, but he didn't say a word. She had enough to worry about that didn't involve his making plans for a future they couldn't have.

"Quint, please tell me." She placed a hand on his cheek.

Her touch burned through him. "I don't know who was here or what they were looking for in that garage. I snuck up on him. He pulled one off, but not before I had my way. That's all you need to know."

She grabbed his hands. "Your knuckles."

"Darlin', stop fussing over me. If you want to reconnect my side, get to it. Otherwise, we need to get back to my truck."

"You're in no position to drive."

"Then you will." He leaned his head back and closed his eyes. The fight ran out of him like a bronco being broken. His side hurt, and the dizziness was winning. They needed to get out of this house before more trouble came that he couldn't handle at the moment.

"Don't move." She ran off into another room and made enough noise that anyone within fifty feet of the house would hear.

He pushed off the couch and groaned. Time to go. She could sew him up later. He should have kept her at the cabin where she would be safe, and he wouldn't have to fight. He didn't want to use his fists on anyone ever again, and tonight he'd run out of choices.

He meant what he said to her earlier about wanting to kill someone if they hurt her. He'd fallen for this woman. Now he couldn't trust himself to walk away in time. That was part of the reason he couldn't work for Hank. He didn't have to love someone for anger to blind him to reason. He hadn't loved Sarah when he killed her husband.

"Cheyenne." His voice scraped his throat.

She spun around from searching the kitchen drawers. "I was looking for thread. Why are you up?"

"You're making more noise than pigs to the slaughter. Fix me up at home. I'll be fine till then." He leaned against the wall and hoped he wouldn't slide to the ground.

"Did you say 'home'?" She checked under the towel he pressed to his side.

"I don't know what I said." He only knew they were wasting time, and it was taking more effort than he had to stay in control of the situation. He would not be able to fight for her a second time tonight.

"You need stitches. I don't want you bleeding for another two hours while we make our way back."

"You can stitch me up on the side of the road someplace. I'm begging you to go."

"Okay."

A flash of light came through the windows and shattered the moment of peace that made space in his lungs.

Someone else was here.

CHAPTER 9

QUINT HAD BEGGED her to go. He was hurt worse than he was letting on. Now she had wasted too much time looking for thread. Someone else was pulling up to the house. If they hurried, they might make it out the back and into the woods to his truck. He would have to lean on her, and she wasn't going to be fast. Not with a man over six feet using her as a crutch.

They were out of choices. She grabbed the notebooks first. She went back to him and wrapped his arm around her shoulders, and linked her arm around his waist, careful not to touch the wound. Without another word, they went out the back door.

She listened for the sound of a car door or voices, but nothing came. The darkness would finally be on their side. She didn't waste time zig-zagging. That might keep them safe, but would do nothing to help Quint. She had to protect him now.

He grunted a few times, but he never said a word.

"Over there," someone yelled. A man, maybe. A voice that could be familiar.

She picked up speed and prayed she wouldn't drop the notebooks. Pounding footsteps chased them.

"We're going the wrong way," Quint said.

"Are you sure?" She kept going.

"You might know medicine, but I know the land." He pulled away from her and stumbled.

She reached for him, but he took her hand and led her to in the opposite direction. Snapping branches littered the air with noise. Their pursuers gained speed, as if they knew what direction she and Quint would take. Quint wouldn't be able to out run them, and without his speed, she couldn't either. Tucker and his men could know where the truck was. Someone could be waiting for them there.

"Are you sure we should go to the truck?" The words forced their way out in between haggard breaths.

"Can't run the whole way back. Need the horse-power." He squeezed her hand.

They crossed the tree line behind the garage. She wanted to stop and catch her breath or check Quint's wound that must be spilling blood like a waterfall, but she kept going. The trees might provide coverage, but they weren't safe yet.

She listened for more footsteps, but only the sounds of nature accented the night. The truck waited under the brush he had covered it with. No one was there waiting with guns. Relief gave her another shot of adrenaline. He grabbed at branches, but he struggled to get them off the hood.

"Stop." She pushed him away, and he didn't argue.

He bent over and gulped in air while she uncovered the truck. She needed to take care of him, but they didn't have time. The best thing they could do was get on the road and find a place to stop where she could stitch him up. She had shoved what she needed into her pockets. Everything was still there.

"Let me help you get in the truck." She wrapped an arm around his waist, but he pushed her away. "Put your pride aside, cowboy. Let me help you."

He grunted and slid into the passenger seat. He handed her the keys. "I'll tell you which way to go. Can you drive a stick?"

"I'm from Montana. Of course, I can."

"Then hurry the hell up about it." He leaned back, but he gripped her hand and gave a squeeze.

She tried to pull her hand away, but he held on. A smile tugged at the corner of his lips. "Forgive me, darlin'. I'm hurting."

"Which way?" Any other time she might let her anger stew, but not now. The man he really was, was the man in her bed last night.

He directed her through the woods until she was on a recognizable road. She turned left and right at his direction and kept her eyes on the rearview mirror as much as out the windshield. No one followed them. Whoever had come back had somehow missed them. The gratitude choked her. She had the man next to her to thank for that. She would have led them in the wrong direction and maybe to their deaths.

"I'm pulling over and taking care of your wound."

"No arguing from me."

It took another ten minutes until she found a side road where the houses were spread far apart and away from the road. She cleaned her hands with bottled water and wished for soap. He held the flashlight while she sterilized the needle with a lighter. He didn't flinch while she worked. She kept her gaze on her job. If she dared to look at him, she would falter. There was something to say about not working on a person you loved. She let out a long breath. The reality smacked her in the chest. She tied a knot and broke off the thread.

"There. You'll be okay now." She tugged his shirt back down.

Sweat beaded on his brow. She kissed his moist lips. He put a hand behind her neck and pulled her close. He pressed his lips to hers with a fierceness he hadn't before. His tongue pushed her lips apart and tangled with hers. She wanted to climb into his lap and have him right away.

He eased back. "Thank you."

"Close your eyes and rest."

"I'll direct us to the road leading to the cabin first." His breathing sounded as if he'd run a marathon.

Each time he gave her directions, it cost him. She wished she knew the way and could let him have some peace.

"Take this road around the bend. About a mile up make a right. The road is not marked, but it's the only turn. That's the way to the cabin. If you see the hospital, you went too far. You got it?"

"I think so."

"Good." He closed his eyes.

The road was nothing more than a tight country road that climbed into the hills. There were no streetlights or sidewalks. Only deer grazed in the grass and a fox darted across the street. They had made it out with the notebooks. Relief straightened her shoulders. Quint could take some time to heal. She'd find a way onto the racetrack property that didn't involve him. He deserved a break.

They had driven a mile since the bend. She didn't see a right-hand turn. A sign for the hospital glowed in the reflection of the headlights. She must've missed the street and turned the truck around. Her heart picked up speed. Now wasn't the time to get lost. Maybe she hadn't driven far enough the first time. She gripped the wheel until her knuckles turned white and circled around for the second time. She followed the road to the hospital. Too far.

She retraced the path and still no turn. She hated to wake him, but grabbed his hand and squeezed. "Quint?"

He didn't respond.

She took her eyes off the road. His head rested against the seat. His mouth opened in a small circle. She reached for his neck to check his pulse.

The truck swerved.

She yanked the wheel. The truck rocked as if it might turn over. Her throat closed up.

"Whoa. I thought you could drive a stick." He grabbed his side.

"I'm sorry. I thought…" Her words stuck to the roof of her mouth.

"You thought what?" He readjusted his position and rested his head against the window. He closed his eyes.

"Never mind." She thought he had died while she wasn't looking. Fear shook her insides. She gripped the steering wheel until her knuckles turned white again.

She had just found him. She couldn't lose him now. He was hurt because of her, and not once had he said as much. He hadn't yelled at her, or cursed her. He would have every right to feel that way. That's what life with her last boyfriend had been like. He blamed her for everything. Every missed opportunity, every mistake. She hadn't thought about him in a while. Her problems had grown from ending a bad relationship to saving her life.

She found the turn and followed the road to the

cabin. She parked the truck as close to the cabin door as possible and jumped from the truck. The cabin appeared as they left it. She unlocked the door and did a quick check. The front room held a chill in it. A fire from the wood-burning stove would chase the cold away.

Quint struggled to get out of the truck. She ran to him and leaned against him to offer support. "I'm fine, darlin'."

"You're a big, fat liar. You need to get some rest." She would take the truck tomorrow and get into those stables by herself. She wasn't going to allow him to come with her, and if that meant tying him to the bed, she would.

A smile tugged on her lips. Now was not the time to think about tying up her sexy cowboy. Hopefully, there would be a chance for some of that later. If he still wanted her, if she could prove Tucker hurt those horses, if she didn't have to run for the rest of her life.

She helped him to the bedroom and sat him on the bed. He smiled at her, and her heart knocked on her ribs. "I'm sorry," she said.

"Nothing to be sorry about. You didn't shoot me."

"It's my fault. I dragged you into this." She tugged his bloody and torn shirt over his head. "I'm just glad the bullet only grazed your side. If it had stuck inside you, we'd have bigger problems." She hadn't asked him what he saw, but that could wait now. In the morning, she'd ask who the person was with the gun.

"A little sleep is all I need. Did you lock the doors?"

"I thought I'd leave the door wide open with a sign inviting Tucker in." She yanked off his boots.

"You're sassing me again. Did anyone follow us after the woods? Did I ask you that?" The circles around his eyes were purple, and the lines around his mouth had deepened.

"You did not and no. Now, lie down. I'm going to find some ibuprofen. I wish I had antibiotics, but I'll keep an eye on you. I'll also grab a warm wash cloth to clean the blood off your skin." She turned to go, but he grabbed her hand.

"The only thing I need is you beside me. Slide into bed." He edged to the far side of the bed and made room for her.

"I'll sleep in the other room. You need to be comfortable."

"My comfort will come from you next to me. Now, don't argue with an injured man." He patted the bed.

A warm rush ran over her skin. "Let me just find the ibuprofen for you."

"Hurry up about it." He flopped back.

She ran around the cabin getting what she needed, but when she returned, Quint snored. She let out a long breath. "The man sleeps."

She covered him with the blanket and left the pills and water by the bed if he woke. She found blankets in the other room and went out to the couch by the fire.

Exhaustion crushed her chest. She pressed the pillow against her face.

And cried.

CHAPTER 10

QUINT WOKE WITH A START. The sudden movement sent a pain up his side. He groaned. His body ached; his side burned, and his pride was spitting mad. He eased up on his elbow. Cheyenne wasn't in the room, and that only managed to light his anger on fire.

The glow of the clock on the bedside table did little to break into the darkness. He had no idea how long he'd been asleep, but she gave him the bed when he had asked her not to. She was caring for him. That should make him happy, but she was a doctor. She would care for any injured animal, including him.

He made a stupid mistake by sneaking up on the guy in her yard without a weapon of some kind. Whoever Tucker had sent, had waited for him out on Cheyenne's father's property. His surprise hadn't been much of one. The guy was ready. They'd fought, and for a minute, he thought he had the upper hand until the man pulled his gun. If he hadn't rolled away at the last second, he would have had a bullet in his chest. It was his last kick to the guy's head that saved his life, or he'd be dead and so would Cheyenne. He couldn't let something like that happen again. He would protect her at all costs as long as he was breathing.

He swung his legs over the bed with a grunt. She had left him the pain reliever, and he swallowed them dry. He needed something stronger and a shot of whiskey. Maybe there was a liquor cabinet somewhere in this place.

His legs wobbled under him, but he forced himself to stand straight and go find his woman. He stopped. She wasn't his or anyone's. She belonged to herself, and if she shared herself with him, he would be the luckiest bastard in the world.

"What are you doing, darlin'?" He found her sitting cross-legged on the couch, wearing his old flannel. She was surrounded by those notebooks. The light beside her cast a yellow glow that only managed to make her look more beautiful. The fire in the woodstove crackled and invited him in the room.

Her gaze snapped up. She pushed the books away and came to him. "Are you okay?"

He folded her in his arms and inhaled her sweet scent mixed with wood smoke. She rested her head against his chest. For the first time in hours, he could breathe.

"I'm fine. Woke up lonely, is all. Are you coming to bed?"

"I like the sound of that, but you won't believe what I found." She pushed away, and he wanted to grab her back, but let her go.

Her eyes shone in the small light. Pride must be filling her up. That look on her face made him want her more.

He folded down onto the couch. "Show me, then."

She held open a notebook and sat beside him. "Are you sure you're okay? You look a little pale."

"You can stop doctoring me now. Go on, tell me what you found."

"My father kept journals. He wanted documentation of what he did for Tucker. He doesn't make any excuses. He had a gambling problem and couldn't get out from under it." Her shoulders sagged. "I didn't know that. He had a disease and didn't tell anyone. It explains a lot."

"Everyone has demons lurking somewhere."

"I guess so. Anyway, he wrote down all the medications he gave Tucker's horses for years. When a horse died unexpectedly, he went back and highlighted the drugs that would have caused it."

"Is that enough proof to put Tucker away?"

She closed the book with a thwack. "I don't think so. Tucker could argue it. I still need that urine sample. That will be proof positive and with the notebooks, I will have him. I might not even need whatever is on the computer, though I'd still like to see it."

"I don't like the idea of you going to the racetrack after what happened tonight. They're watching for you and probably hoping you'll show up there. Give the notebooks to Hank. Let him do something with them, and get out of this."

She put a hand on his thigh. Her touch made his center simmer. "I can't. I have to see this to the end. Tucker ruined my reputation. I'll never be able to work in our town again if I can't be the one to prove he did it. Everyone will always wonder if what he said was true if Hank comes to my rescue."

"I'll take you to the track even if I won't like it." Reason and logic dried up like a harvest without water when he was around this woman. It's how he ended up shot tonight and how he ended up in jail. He was playing with fire and couldn't step away.

"I want you to stay here tomorrow and rest. You could rip open that wound. You've done enough for me already. More than enough." Her hand moved farther up his leg.

He laced his fingers through hers before she went any further. Not that he didn't want her, but he wanted to clean up first for her. "You aren't going alone to those stables. Don't argue with me about it. We'll wait till sundown, and I'll drive you. You can get that sample while I keep watch." He wished he had a gun for the first time in a long time.

"Quint, I can handle it. I'll come straight back here after I drop the sample off to the lab."

He cupped her face so he could hold her gaze. "You'll do no such thing. I don't care how capable you are. I want to protect you, and I can't do that from here." He placed a kiss on her lips. She tasted like honey. "Tell me you won't sneak out when I'm not looking."

She wrapped her arms around his neck and moved closer. "You want to protect me?"

"Yes, ma'am."

She tangled her fingers into the back of his hair. The buzz of desire traveled south. He forgot about the pain in his side and focused on the pressure against his zipper.

"Even though I don't need you to, I like the sound of that." Her breath warmed and soothed his skin.

"I know you don't really need me, but I have some strength your beautiful body doesn't have, and I have some skills my training gave me. I can be of use to you." He kissed her neck. He couldn't stop himself. He needed to taste more of her.

She leaned into him and moaned. "That feels nice, but you should stop."

He jumped back as if he'd been burned. He never had to be asked twice to stop. He dropped his hands to his sides. "Did I do something wrong?"

"Just the opposite, but what kind of a woman would

I be if I tried to make love to an injured man hours after he'd been shot?"

He moved over her, and she leaned back against the couch. They were inches apart. He shifted her legs so he could lay between them. She stared up at him with laughter in her eyes. Her black hair fanned out over the cushion. "The kind I want underneath me. But not tonight."

The laughter died in her eyes. "You are hurt. We should we go to the hospital."

"I don't need the hospital. I need a long, hot shower. I can't make love to you smelling like a horse."

She ran her fingers over his jaw. The amusement returned to her gaze. "I'm a vet. I love the smell of horses."

A laugh built low in his belly and rumbled out. He grabbed her leg and wrapped it around his waist. "Just remember you said that."

He kissed her, not wanting to wait another second. He pushed her lips apart with his tongue to take the kiss deeper and she rewarded him with a sigh.

He wanted to hurry and slow down at the same time. This woman gave herself to him willingly. She acted as if he was the only man who could make her feel this way. She didn't cringe at his touch the way Sarah had. Cheyenne's hands explored his body avoiding the stitches on his side. Her gentle touch filled his chest with warmth.

He fumbled with the buttons on her flannel shirt,

wanting to get it out of his way. She took her hands off his body to help him. She pushed the fabric aside and pressed her skin to his. Her soft curves filled in his straight lines.

He dropped his mouth to her breast for a sweet taste. She arched into him, and his desire for her filled his head with a maddening frenzy. His hands searched her body then lingered on her hip. He could stay like this all night and be happy.

She grabbed his hand off her hip and placed it on the breast being ignored. He met her gaze. "You trying to tell me something?"

"Should I spell it out?"

"Don't read much." He mapped out a trail of kisses down her stomach and caught the top of her panties between his teeth.

She gasped as he tugged the lace until it tore. His tongue ran along her leg until he found the center of her heat. He wanted to bring her all the pleasure she created in him. He would never be able to let Cheyenne go after tonight. She had found a way into his soul.

He tested her readiness with a flick of his tongue, and she moaned her approval. Pride puffed up his chest. She surrendered to the touch of his mouth on her most intimate space while his hands ran over her body.

She gripped his hands. "Quint, please come back up here."

"Why do you want me to stop?"

"Because I want you inside me, now." She stroked the full length of him.

Her touch brought him to the edge. He kissed her again, hoping she would know what he felt for her. He was in the arms of an angel.

She wrapped her legs around his waist and guided their bodies in line. He moved her hand so he could enter her. He soared as she rocked her hips with his.

Being with her set him free. He was like a wild horse running across the plains. He was not handcuffed to his past or his bad choices. With Cheyenne, he could be the man he wanted to be.

She cried out his name. Her muscles flexed around him as her body shuddered with the end of her release. He met her then, driven to the end by her pleasure. His chest heaved and his side hurt again, but that didn't matter.

He bundled her in his arms.

"I love you," she said.

"Me too, darlin'. Me too."

CHAPTER 11

CHEYENNE TRIED to shake off her nerves, but it wasn't working. In a few hours, she would have Dark Matter's urine sample, and she would be able to prove without a doubt that Tucker tried to force her to inject his horse with anabolic steroids. It would be the end of him, and the end of her having to fear for her life. She might even be able to practice again.

She shoved her father's computer into her backpack. She still hadn't figured out the password. She had tried every stupid thing she could think of. He was probably the first person in history not to use a personal name as a password.

"Quint, are you ready?"

A rush of heat ran over her skin. Her cheeks burned thinking about the intimate moments they shared last night. They had made love several times. She couldn't keep her hands or her tongue off him.

She hadn't meant to say she loved him. It had slipped out while she glowed from her orgasm. But he hadn't pushed her away. He hadn't said it exactly, but a man like Quint who kept to himself, would find it difficult to declare such emotion.

He came into the living room, favoring his injured side. He shoved his hands into his back pockets of his ripped jeans. "I was thinking we should forget about the race track."

"What? Why?"

"Are you sure you can't prove what Tucker did from those notebooks?"

"I need ironclad proof. I won't back down now. I'm too close." She yanked the zipper of the backpack closed and slung it over her shoulder.

"Let it go. Give Hank or the Montana Board of Horse Racing the evidence you already have. You can keep your head down and stay alive." He came closer.

"What's this really about?" She backed up.

"I told you. I want you to stop fighting, and let someone else take the risk. If you keep your head down and stay out of trouble, you'll have a chance."

"You can't live your life on the sidelines." She never thought he'd ask her to run away. He was fearless risking his life for her, and now he allowed fear to get in the way of what she needed.

"We're not talking about me right now. You don't have to take this on anymore."

"I'm standing up for what's right. I thought you of

all people could understand that."

"Standing up isn't always worth it. I did that, and I ended up in jail. I ruined my life. You could end up dead. Is that what you want?" His voice climbed to the ceiling.

"I'm willing to take the risk. Tucker can't get away with what he's been doing and what he did to my dad." Fire burned in her veins. After all they shared, he was asking her to back down. He didn't understand her at all, and if that was the case, maybe he couldn't really love her.

He ran a hand over his face and stayed mute.

She wanted to shake him. "If you hadn't hit that man in the bar, you wouldn't be standing here with me. If every stupid thing I've done so far is the reason I'm with you now, I'd do it all again."

She stomped out of the cabin and waited by the truck. She would count to ten, okay twenty, and if he wasn't outside, she'd go alone. She had pocketed the keys while he was busy being an ass.

"Cheyenne?"

She turned her back and crossed her arms over her chest. His words had hollowed her heart even if he didn't mean his ruined life included her. They had only been together a few days. Still, tears pricked her eyes.

He placed his hands on her shoulders. "I don't want anything to happen to you. I wouldn't survive if it did."

She turned to face him. "What are you saying?"

"Darlin', you know what I'm saying. If you're determined to take on this fight, then I'll help you. Now, give me the keys you swiped." He held out his hand.

"You saw me do that?" She dropped the keys in his palm.

He held the truck door open for her. "You're not much of a pickpocket."

"Thank you for believing in me." She settled into the seat and let the warmth of his being next to her wash over her.

"I'll be glad when this is all over and we can go back to our regular lives." He turned the truck around and headed down the mountain.

She hoped he meant together. If proving Tucker Gray wrong meant losing Quint, she was going to have one long, lonely life.

CHEYENNE HAD a little over twenty-four hours to get Dark Matter's urine sample returned from the lab. By that time, she could have her life back. What little there was of it.

Quint parked the truck across the street from the Waterpark Race Track behind a strip mall with more vacant space than stores. At this late hour, the horse would be tucked in, and most everyone would be asleep.

They would have to sneak onto the racetrack property and into the horse barn. Her nerves agreed with

Quint's idea to leave this all behind. If they were caught, Tucker would kill them both.

Quint grabbed the bucket and glass jar out of the truck. "How often does he take a pee?"

"I have to walk him."

"Oh, hell no." He stopped.

"I have a catheter in my backpack. I'd rather not use that because I don't want him to kick me."

"Is there a tap we could run?" Quint took her hand and walked around to the front of the strip mall.

The place was dark and deserted. Even the lights at the racetrack were out. They could use the jockey entrance and circle around to the horse barn.

"I don't remember where the hoses are. If there are hoses nearby, and the catheter doesn't work, then we'll try that. Otherwise, I have to walk him."

"I can't let you do that. Someone will see us. Put the bucket under him and we'll wait. He's going to be hydrated. It might not be long."

"I'm not sitting there all night. I want that sample, and I want to get the hell out of there."

"You thinking I was right about giving this up?" He stared down at her with a glint in his eye.

She shoved him. "Shut up. I'm scared enough as it is."

He laughed and pulled her close. "You are one spunky lady. That's a good quality. Now, take my hand and stay close. I want this over as much as you do. More."

He led her across the street and up the long drive to the jockey entrance. They stayed close to the tree line that blocked this area from the parking lot. A dorm for the jockeys was to the left. The lights were out in all of the windows except one.

The road banked to the right. The enormous race-track reached for the sky with its four seating levels. Tomorrow the whole place would be filled with people betting on a favorite horse for sport or fun. Or worse, to try to get ahead of their debt, the way her father would have. His journals said that was how the gambling started. He was a racehorse vet who thought he knew the inside scoop. Only he hadn't.

The barn came into view. Her lungs held onto what little air they had. She gripped Quint's hand.

"You've come this far." He tugged her forward.

He was right. She couldn't turn around now. She smiled up at him. "Thank you. I know you don't want me doing this."

"No, I don't. I don't like this one bit. But you're determined even if you're frightened, and I won't get in the way of that. You'll regret the decision to walk away, and I won't have you blaming me. I'll do whatever it takes to keep you safe. I just don't like what that might be."

She wanted to kiss him for his protectiveness, but she would have to wait until later. "I'll be quick. We don't need a big sample."

They approached the barn. She expected to find a

horse rider or a groomer around, but the place was empty except for the horses. They caught a break.

"You stay at the door and watch. I'll take care of Dark Matter," she said.

"Are you sure you don't need help? He's a big horse, and there's not a lot of room in that stall." He handed over the bucket.

"I'll be fine." She leaned up and kissed him after all.

Dark Matter's stall was the last one on the right. The stable held ten other horses. One snorted and picked its head up as she went by. The barn smelled of ammonia and hay. She pulled the flashlight from the backpack. Its bouncing, thin beam was all the light she'd have to work with. She hoped it would be enough.

"Hey, boy." She approached the stall with caution. The horse would pick up on her nerves. It had been months since she'd seen him. She didn't have carrots. That was a mistake she should not have made. She tried a long, slow breath.

Dark Matter's eyes were wide, and he retracted his lips.

"You don't have to be afraid. It's Doc Locklear. Remember?" She controlled her voice to stay calm even though her heart raced to find a way out of her chest.

The horse pinned back his ears. She came closer, but he struck the stall door. She jumped back. "Okay, you aren't happy about my being here." How long had he been showing signs of aggressive behavior?

He was used to people, and horses didn't typically show dominance toward humans. She had been away, but not so long he wouldn't remember her. That meant the steroids were changing his behavior, and very possibly Tucker upped the dosage.

She should go right back to Quint. Dark Matter wasn't going to allow her to catheter him. But she had to try. She opened the stall door. He snorted and raised his tail.

"It's okay. We're friends." She stroked his nose, but he turned his head.

There wasn't a lot of room to move around. She clamped the flashlight between her teeth and removed the catheter from the backpack. Thankfully, her father taught her to keep a few supplies handy. She edged closer to the back of the horse.

Her heart continued to hammer against her chest. Her hands shook. "You won't even feel this."

Her training screamed in her head to get out of the stall. She knew better as a vet. Dark Matter was angry, but she would not allow Tucker to get away with what he was doing and what he did to her father and her. If she didn't stop him, who else would he ruin? How many more horses would die under his ownership? He had to be stopped, and she was the only one who could do it.

She inserted the catheter. Dark Matter's piercing whinny shrilled through the barn.

The last thing she saw, before the world went black, was the horse's leg coming right for her.

QUINT RAN FOR THE STALL. The horse's trumpet-like neigh meant only one thing. He slid to a stop. Dark Matter snorted and stomped his front legs. Cheyenne lay slumped in the corner out cold. Blood ran down her face. His stomach hollowed out.

"Easy, boy." He held his hands up. He had to get the horse out of the stall before he could get in there and grab Cheyenne.

He clicked his tongue a few times. Dark Matter turned his head in the direction of the sound. He looked around for some hay and took a couple of slow steps to the bale beside the stall. He offered some as a treat.

Dark Matter nosed the hay. Quint whistled and backed up. Racehorses were well trained and very used to having their needs met. Dark Matter took a step in Quint's direction.

"That's it, boy. Come on out. I need to get my lady."

He grabbed a nearby bucket and shoved more hay into the pail. Dark Matter went to the food. Tucker must have cut back on food to make him run faster. Quint eased into the stall, scooped up Cheyenne, gathered her things, and ran.

CHAPTER 12

QUINT DEPOSITED Cheyenne on the front seat of the truck. His lungs burned, and his breath came in short bursts. The blood ran down the side of her head. Her lip was swollen and bleeding. She should look a lot worse if Dark Matter kicked her square in the face. She was unresponsive, maybe a concussion, but at least she was breathing.

He wanted to kill Gray, and when this was over, he was going to do just that. If he spent the rest of his life in jail, he didn't give a fuck.

"Hang on, darlin'. I'm going to get help." He dumped her belongings on the floor in front of her and ran around the front of the truck.

He sped out onto the road and kicked up dirt. He raced through every red light and laid on his horn to alert other drivers to stay the fuck out of his way. She hadn't moved. He gripped her shoulder and squeezed. "Don't die on me."

His vision blurred with rage. He shook his head to clear his sight and turned the corner on two wheels. He fumbled for his phone and tapped at the screen. The truck swerved. He yanked the wheel back.

"Montero." Jax's voice came through the speaker.

"It's Quint. Cheyenne needs a doctor. She might have been kicked by a horse."

"Can you get to the hospital?"

"She's supposed to stay hidden."

"I'll take care of that. When you get to the hospital, drive around to the back at the service entrance. Can you get there or do I need to come to you?"

"I can get there. In twenty minutes."

"We'll be waiting." Jax ended the call.

No questions asked. He owed them, and he knew what the price would be. He floored it the rest of the way.

The truck bounced over the entrance to the hospital parking lot. His front bumper scraped the asphalt. He reached out and grabbed Cheyenne even though he had buckled her seatbelt. Blood matted her hair. He was going to lose her.

An ambulance, with its spinning lights, deposited someone by the emergency room entrance. He sped past that and around to the back of the red brick hospital. The truck fishtailed as he slammed on the brakes.

Jax and another man came running. Quint jumped out of the truck.

"What happened?" Jax threw open the passenger door. Together, they eased Cheyenne out and onto a gurney.

"I don't know exactly. The horse squealed. I ran. She was out by the time I got there."

The other man, tall with hair to his shoulders and a beard, pushed the gurney up the ramp as he and Jax ran beside her.

"Who are you?" He had to know who else he was going to owe after this.

"Lincoln Smith. I'm Jax's partner and here to help in any way I can."

They ran through a series of hallways. He wouldn't remember the way if he had to. Jax burst through a set of double doors into an operating room with white tiled walls, bright lights, an operating table, and a bald man waiting in scrubs.

"Quint, this is Dr. Buckstone. He's going to take care of Cheyenne," Jax said.

"How is this all possible?" He couldn't believe what he saw.

"It's the Brotherhood." Lincoln patted him on the shoulder.

"Is this your wife?" Dr. Buckstone lifted Cheyenne's eyelids and pointed a light at her.

"Uh, no, sir." If she survived this, he would get down on his knee and beg her to marry his sorry ass.

"This isn't a horse kick." The doctor continued to examine her. "Her face would be shattered somewhere. I've seen it before. I'll take her in for x-rays and CT scans. Why don't you wait in the waiting room? I'll come find you when I know more."

Jax ushered him out into the hall before he could protest. He wanted to stay with her.

"It's okay, man. He's the best. You want something to drink?" Jax brought him to a small room with two sofas, several straight-backed chairs, a table filled with wrinkled magazines, and a television stuck to the wall.

"Nah." He paced the small room. The space smelled like bleach and lemon.

"I can get you a beer," Lincoln said.

"Okay, then." He needed something to help calm his nerves, or he might punch a hole through the wall.

"All you can do now is wait." Jax dropped down on the couch.

"I need to do something." He continued to pace.

"Man, you're going to wear out the floor. Doc Buckstone is the best. Have a seat." Jax pointed to the chair.

He stood.

Lincoln came back with three beers. He drank his while the two men talked about life as if they weren't waiting in a hospital. Any other time, he might think about hanging with these guys, but now all he could do was hope Cheyenne would come back to him.

"Did you ever get that computer working?" Lincoln's voice dragged him out of his thoughts.

"She can't figure it out."

"Any chance you have it with you?"

"It's out in the truck. In a backpack." He wasn't going anywhere. No one better ask.

"I'll grab it." Lincoln tossed his beer can in the trash and went out the door.

How much longer would he have to wait? What was going on in there? He would go back and demand some answers. He turned for the door.

"You really need to sit down," Jax said.

"I'm going to ask you real polite to stop asking me to sit." He clenched his fists.

Jax laughed and shook his head. "Yeah, you'll fit in just fine."

Some of the anger seeped out of his veins. He ran a hand over his face and scratched his jaw. Cheyenne would want him to hold it together. "How long have you worked for Hank?"

"A long time. You'll like it. It's a place for you to work out that anger of yours. A lot of the guys left the military hurt, confused, and frustrated. They don't always know what life is going to be like for them. Hank knows what we all need. He's a former Navy SEAL. He gets it."

"I don't want to give up my life on the ranch."

"You don't have to completely. Ty will give you the time off when you need it. His father and Hank go way back. Ty is Lincoln's brother-in-law, in fact. We're one big family. For me, the Brotherhood is as important as my siblings or my wife and kid."

A family. That was something he hadn't had in a very long time. When his father left, he never came back. It was only him and his mom until she died without any warning. Then Sarah left him and he landed in jail. Working with Ty and the ranchers was the closest thing he had to a family, and he always kept them at a distance. There was no more space for heartbreak.

Until Cheyenne showed up and blew his heart wide open with possibilities. He couldn't lose her now. He clenched his fists again. Nothing better happen to her.

Dr. Buckstone came into the waiting room. The bright lights shone off his head. Jax stood. Quint tried not to grab the doctor by the shirt and shake the news out of him.

"She's going to be fine." Buckstone's smile spread wide.

"Are you sure?" A rush of air left his lungs. He dropped into the chair with a thud.

"It's a concussion and a few abrasions on her face. She's conscious now. She jumped out of the way of the horse's leg at the last second. Good reflexes. But in her haste, she collided with the metal framing of the barn. That's tornado sturdy. She's lucky she didn't break her neck with that kind of force."

"But all that blood, and the stall was too small to

move around in." He would never get the image of her curled up and bleeding out of his head.

"Head wounds bleed a lot. I gave her ten stitches and some pain medicine for the headache and the bruises on her face. She might have come down on a shovel. The cut looks that way and she thought she saw a shovel in the stall."

He hadn't even noticed the shovel because all he could think about was saving her. She had saved herself. If he was a praying man, he would say one now. "Can I see her?"

"For a short time. She should rest. I want to keep her overnight for observation."

"Thank you." He stuck his hand out.

The doctor looked at his hand then back up at him. "You don't need to thank me. It's my honor to help out the Brotherhood. Thank you for your service." Dr. Buckstone shook his hand.

"Linc and I will wait for you. Take your time." Jax pointed toward the door.

"I can never repay you for setting up all this and saving her." The words stuck in his throat. "I'll call Hank in the morning and tell him I accept the job."

"Don't worry about that now. I can give him the message. Go be with your woman. We'll be here when you're done." Jax sat back down and pulled out his phone.

Quint ran after the doctor.

"Now, don't be alarmed by the bruising. She'll look

good as new in a few days." Buckstone stopped at a closed door. "This is our special wing for very private cases. We had a celebrity deliver her baby here once."

There were only five doors in the hallway and a nurses' station in the middle. A man in blue scrubs sat behind the counter typing at a computer.

"Parker, Mr. Porter will be visiting with Doctor Locklear for a little while," Buckstone said.

"Got it." Parker gave a thumbs-up.

"Go on in." Buckstone went back up the hall the way they came.

On a long breath, Quint pushed open the door. The room was dark except for a small light over the bed. The blankets swallowed Cheyenne. Her eyes were closed. A large, white bandage covered half of her head. Her face was several shades of purple. Someone had cleaned the blood off her face and out of her hair.

Relief expanded his heart until it didn't fit in his chest. Or maybe that was something more. He walked up to the bed the way he might approach a scared colt. The floor squeaked under his step.

She turned her head. A smile spread across her face. "Hi."

He cleared the rest of the space in two steps and took her hand in his. "Hey, darlin'. How are you feeling?"

"Better now that you're here."

The power of those words shoved him into the chair beside the bed. "I'm sorry I wasn't with you in the barn. I should have been with you. I could have done something. I would have known the horse was going to kick. You were too close to the whole thing trying to prove Tucker was behind the steroids. You must've missed the signs. Not on purpose, 'cause you're a good doctor, but —"

"Quint, you're rambling." She squeezed his hand.

He clamped his mouth shut. He was going on as if he was some old lady gossiping at church. "I'm just glad you're okay." He had been scared when the horse called out. He was never so scared in his whole life. Not even while in jail.

He kissed her knuckles. He wanted to kiss her everywhere just to prove to himself she really would be fine. But her lip was swollen, and she had a bandage under her chin. Dark circles covered her eyes. She was still beautiful to him.

"Will you stay with me tonight? I don't want to be here alone."

"I won't leave your side unless you tell me to." He didn't care what the doctor said. He wasn't leaving. He would tell Jax to go home without him.

"Is there any chance you took my backpack?" She ran her thumb over the top of his hand.

"I didn't want to waste the time gathering your stuff, but I didn't want any trace of you left behind."

"I might have taken a sample. The catheter went in, and then Dark Matter kicked. I might still have a chance."

"The catheter was on the ground. You didn't get anything."

She closed her eyes. One tear slid down her cheek. He wiped it away. "All of that for nothing. You were right. I should've stayed in the cabin. Instead, I'm lying in a hospital bed with no way to prove Tucker injected those horses."

"We'll find something else." His heart broke in half.

"There's no point. I can give the notebooks to the authorities, but then I'll have to start over somewhere else far from here. If Tucker finds someone else to do his bidding, maybe he'll forget about me."

"You don't have to run. I'll keep you safe. I'm taking that job with Hank. You'll never have to worry about Tucker." Because he could not lose her. The idea shook him to his core.

She put a hand on his face. He kissed her palm.

"You're such a good man. When I look at you, I see strength and honor. You growl at the world, but with me you are sweet and tender. I love that most about you. You save that small part of yourself for me. But I can't ask you to watch out for me forever. What I did to you wasn't fair. As soon as I'm released, I'll go and let you get back to the life you want." Her eyes filled with tears.

His own tears burned the back of his throat. He grasped her hand in both of his, closed his eyes, and took a deep breath. His impulses had always brought him trouble, but this time he wanted the woman in front of him. He was willing to jump without thinking. She was the light in a dark world. He locked his gaze on her.

"Cheyenne, I know I don't have a lot to offer someone like you. But I will spend every day making you happy, if you'll let me. Marry me."

"Quint, I—"

"You aren't going to believe this." Jax burst through the door. Lincoln was fast on his heels. He held the computer in one hand with the top open.

The smile on their faces said they found good news.

So, why did he want to punch them both?

CHAPTER 13

"I FIGURED OUT THE PASSWORD." Lincoln held up the computer.

Quint dropped her hand and stood. The scowl had returned to his face. The men's timing was bad, but she couldn't believe the turn of luck. Just when she thought she had lost her chance to prove Tucker was a scumbag, she might get another chance with what could be on that computer.

She struggled to sit up. "How did you do that?"

"Linc is the best. He could figure anything out." Jax slapped Lincoln on the back.

Lincoln laughed and placed the computer in her lap. Quint propped the pillows behind her.

"You want to do this now? If you don't feel up to it, we'll wait." He stared down at her.

She loved him. There was no question about that. She loved the determination in his stare. She loved the way he would protect her from anything. She also loved the scruff that dusted his jaw, the flannel shirt that fit to his chest, and the ripped jeans. But she had to finish what she started. Then and only then could she answer his question with honesty.

"I'm fine. I'd like to see what's on here."

He gave her the smallest of nods.

Lincoln stood at the end of the bed. "I pulled up every piece of information we could find on your dad. I was surprised at how much we located. Between me and my program, we came up with a few possible combinations to unlock the computer. The password is the address of his first vacation home."

"The one in Backwater?"

"Um, no. Your father owned a home in Utah near Cedar Creek. He lost it in a poker game. You would never have come up with that address. As far as we can tell, he never told your mother about owning the house. We aren't sure what he did with it while he owned it, but it must've been important to him."

Her father had a secret life because of the gambling. How many other things lurked in dark corners that she never knew about? "Did he have another family in that house?"

Jax stood beside Lincoln. "We don't know. We can't find anything that says he did, but we found some records of utilities. He might've rented it out for income, but we're not sure."

"He had a gambling problem before I was even born. How did he hide it for so long?" Everything she knew about her father was a lie. He had been the man who told her Quint wasn't good enough for her. That one date was too many and she needed to stay away from him. He had judged everyone who wasn't in his small clique of friends and colleagues as if he were some king on a throne. She had believed him. Worshipped him even. She had wanted to be just like him. Which was why she became a vet. Her stomach churned, and her head throbbed.

"Addicts are very good at hiding their problems. As long as he could pay the debt, no one had to know," Lincoln said.

"My guess is, when he got in over his head, the house of cards fell apart," Jax said. "We're going to let you rest. Quint, if you need anything else, just call. And take as long as you need for Cheyenne. Hank won't put you on assignment until this is all resolved."

Quint nodded. The men left them alone with plenty of unanswered questions hanging in the air.

"I'm going to hunt down some food. Are you hungry?" Quint pushed off the wall.

"No, thank you. I'm going to search through his computer for a little while even though I'm not supposed to look at a screen with my concussion." She should say something about his proposal, but the words didn't come. She couldn't explain her choices without it all coming out wrong. When she was ready to say yes, and if he still wanted her, then she would answer him.

"I won't be gone long." He kissed the top of her head and walked out.

The room was too empty without him. She clicked the keys and moved from one screen to another. The computer was filled with files of all sizes. She wouldn't be able to read everything tonight. Her eyes burned and her head continued to beat out a bad tune on her skull.

She wished Quint would come back. He wouldn't leave her until she was out of the hospital, but would he stay with her after that? Not if she declined his proposal. His pride would never survive.

She opened a folder labeled *audio*.

A dozen files popped up on the screen. She clicked on the oldest one. Her father's voice filled the room. Her hands shook while she listened. As each recording ended, she went onto the next. Sweat ran in a line down her back.

Quint came back in the room carrying a tray of food. He stopped and stared. "Everything okay?"

"I found it. I found the proof."

"STAY IN BED." Quint gripped Cheyenne's arms. This stubborn woman was going to injure herself all over again.

"I have to get dressed. Are my clothes here?" She pushed past him and stood on wobbling legs. "Whoa." She held her head in her hand.

"Please sit." His nerves frayed like an old rope. He was minutes from tying her to the bed. He didn't care if he sounded like a brute. He wanted her to heal even if she didn't want to marry him.

He hadn't missed the way the light went out in her eyes when he asked. It had been a stupid thing to do. She wouldn't want to spend her life with him. What she felt for him had more to do with fear than anything real. He'd forgotten who he was for a minute. Probably because of her. And because of her, he now had a job he didn't want. But he always paid his debts. He'd work for Hank as long as it took to repay the way he helped her.

"Cheyenne, there is nothing you can do tonight. I'll take you anywhere you want tomorrow. Just get back in that bed and rest, damn it."

She flinched.

"I'm sorry." He stepped away from her.

She came up behind him and wrapped her arms around his waist. She placed her cheek against his back. Her soft curves eased the pain in his chest. He laced his fingers through hers.

"If I had the urine sample too, I could really nail Tucker."

"You have all you need right in that computer. Don't

tempt fate by messing with that horse again. You won't be as lucky next time."

"I don't mean to make this difficult. I have to get those files to someone tonight. I need to stop that race tomorrow." Her warm breath heated his skin right through his shirt.

He turned to face her. "Who do you want to give those files to? Are you going to bang on the commissioner's door?"

"Why are you fighting me on this?" She stepped back.

"Because I'm tired of chasing trouble away from your door."

"You don't have to do that anymore. I can take it from here."

"How are you going to keep yourself safe while you stir up the biggest hornet's nest this side of the Continental Divide? What's the plan? You going to steal another horse and gallop in with your computer?" He dropped into the chair. His body ached. He wanted to lie beside her for a few hours and sleep. Things would look different in the light of day. He could come up with a better plan then.

"I don't know who to bring those files to, but I'll figure it out." She tugged on the closet door and dropped the hospital gown to the floor.

Other than her lacy panties, she was naked. His breath caught in his throat. She held his gaze as if to dare him to cross the room. He thought about it for a second, but he wouldn't risk the slap across his face if he tried to change her mind with sex.

She shoved her legs into her jeans splattered with blood. "I don't have a shirt. The doctor must've cut it off me. Give me yours."

"You want me to go shirtless?"

"Well, I certainly can't. Or I could." She fisted her hands on her hips and gave him an eyeful of her breasts.

He stomped across the room and grabbed her by the waist. "Don't even think about walking out of this room half dressed." What she showed him was for his eyes only.

She held out her hand.

He gave her his shirt. He wanted to beg her to stay, but the determined glare shone in her eyes. He had lost this fight.

"You're relieved of your protection duties, Quint Porter. Don't follow me." She scooped up her backpack, shoved in the computer, and pushed through the door.

It swung shut, mocking him.

He picked up the chair and threw it against the window.

It bounced back and landed on the floor. In one piece.

Unlike him.

CHAPTER 14

CHEYENNE PAID the taxi driver and watched as he drove away. The racetrack was only a quarter-mile up the road. If she ignored the pain in her head, she would be okay. This time she had some carrots for Dark Matter, thanks to the convenience store near the hospital. She wouldn't make the same mistakes twice.

She wished Quint was with her, but she set her fate when she marched out on him. He would keep her safer than she could keep herself. He had pissed her off, and she overreacted. He was just trying to help her in the only way he knew how. She couldn't expect him to be any other way. She didn't even want him to be any other way. Her heart ached as much as her head. She should've stayed in bed and let him hold her all night.

The road was dark, and there were no sidewalks. She stayed in the space where the asphalt met the grass line. An owl hooted somewhere in the distance and made her jump. She still had a couple of hours before the sun kissed the sky. There was nothing to be afraid of. The darkness would protect her while she went back to the barn.

She followed the same path she and Quint took earlier past the jockey dorms. Some of the rooms had lights on inside. Jockeys were getting ready for the early morning practice, while others were probably just getting back from a night of drinking.

Her heart raced as she got closer to the horse barn. Her mouth dried out. She licked her lips and groaned. Her bottom lip was swollen from the fall against the shovel. Her reflexes were slow because of the concussion. Going into that stall again was a risk. She had probably lost Quint for good, so taking her chances with an aggressive horse didn't seem so bad.

She took several deep breaths outside the barn door. The roar of an engine and the beam of lights shattered the quiet of the night. She dove for the side of the barn to hide in its shadow.

A door slammed, but the lights prevented her from making out the person.

"Cheyenne, damn it. Have you lost your fucking mind?"

QUINT DIDN'T CARE that he would wake up everyone in a two-mile radius with his hollering. If the world came running, then Cheyenne wouldn't go sticking a needle in that damn horse. He would throw her over his shoulder and drag her back to that cabin, and she wouldn't come out until her bruises were healed.

He marched over to the spot where she flung herself. She jumped into his arms, almost knocking him over. He held her close and inhaled the sweet smell of her hair. "You scared the hell out of me, darlin'."

She gripped him tighter around the neck. "I'm sorry. I should've listened to you. This was a crazy idea. I'll take what I have to the racing board tomorrow. Then I'll walk away."

He eased back to look at her. "You mean that?" He stayed away from the edge of hope. He didn't want to fall to his death.

She nodded.

He pressed his lips to her cheek, avoiding her swollen lips. "Thank you."

"How did you know I was here?"

"Wasn't too hard to figure out."

"You found another shirt to wear?" She ran a hand over his sweatshirt.

He laughed. "I keep a duffel bag in the back of my truck with extra in case a pretty lady steals my clothes."

"I'm not sorry about that. I like you without your clothes on."

"Let's go home."

Cold metal pressed against the back of his skull.

The click of a revolver barrel turning echoed in his ear. Fear turned his belly to ice water.

"Don't move."

He held his hands up. He tried to tell Cheyenne with his eyes to run, but she stood frozen. Her mouth gaped open.

"Tucker," she said.

CHAPTER 15

SHE COULDN'T BELIEVE her eyes. Even after she blinked a few times, Tucker Gray still stood there holding a gun to Quint's head. Tucker, with his receding hairline and weathered skin, wore expensive jeans and boots. A monster like him shouldn't look like a regular guy with money and power.

"Let him go. He has nothing to do with this." Her voice shook.

"That's the thing, Cheyenne. He has everything to do with this. Because when I kill him, you'll finally be my vet again." He cracked his gum as if this was a regular conversation.

"There are a million other vets who want to work for you. Why do you care so much about me?"

"You're hurting my feelings. We're a family. Your father worked for me for years. He wanted you to have his business. Besides, you know how I like my horses taken care of. I can't have you sharing my secrets." He gripped Quint's shoulder and started backing up.

"You don't want this fight," Quint said. "Walk away and she'll forget about the injections."

"Thanks for the advice, but I'm the one with the gun. Since, they don't issue guns to ex-cons in Montana, I'd say with some certainty you don't have one right now."

"Let him go, Tucker. I'll do whatever you want. Does Dark Matter need something tonight? I'll take care of it." She needed to get Tucker's attention away from Quint.

"The first race is at noon. I want him injected right before so his knees don't give him any trouble while he's running."

"Great. Let Quint go; I'll do it."

"Oh, no. He's my guarantee you won't run off again." He slammed the gun into Quint's head. He tumbled to the ground.

She dove. "Quint."

Tucker pointed the gun at her. "Back up."

She scrambled back on her knees. "Don't hurt him. He has nothing to do with this."

"You brought him into this. All you had to do was what I asked. And when you couldn't do that, you should have stayed home and let my men take care of their business. But you ran off, and right to him." Tucker grabbed Quint by the collar and dragged him. "Let's go, or I'll shoot him on the spot."

She followed in defeat. She had ruined everything. All she could do now was keep Quint alive. Tucker would never allow her to live after what she did. After she injected Dark Matter, he'd kill her.

Tucker stopped outside a ground stable barn that leaned to one side. He unlatched the door and pointed the gun at her head. "Inside."

He deposited Quint on the concrete floor by a beam that supported the empty hay loft above. Blood covered the back of his head.

The barn was used for livestock once. Other than rope and some buckets, the place was empty and far enough away from the rest of the area no one would know they were here.

"Can I take a look at his head?" She reached for the backpack. The realization she didn't have it smacked her in the face.

"You can tie him to that pole." Tucker threw a rope at her.

"I'm not going anywhere without him. He doesn't need to be tied up." She threw the rope back at him.

"Honey, I'm going to tie you up too. Now tie him up or I'm going to blow what's left of that pretty face right off your skull." He held the gun an inch from her face and continued to crack his gum.

She propped Quint against the pole. Sweat ran into her eyes, and her stomach threatened to eject whatever content it held. She tied his hands behind the pole.

"Over there." Tucker motioned toward the other beam.

She slid down against the pole so her legs were out in front of her. Tucker squatted down and yanked her arms behind her back. His high-end cologne hinted at her. She kept her gaze forward and tried not to vomit. The rope bit into her wrists as he tugged and pulled.

"I'll be back in a few hours. If you're nice to me, I might even bring some breakfast." He shoved the gun in his holster and left.

"Quint?"

His head hung on his neck like a limp doll.

She struggled against the rope.

What the hell was she going to do now?

CHAPTER 16

THE HEAT in the barn made it difficult to breathe. The sun was high in the sky and cooking them like chicken in a fryer. Sweat slicked Cheyenne's skin, but it did nothing to loosen the rope around her wrists. She had struggled for hours. Her wrists stung more and more with each move. Blood dripped between her fingers, but she couldn't give up.

Quint was still out. He should have come to by now. She hoped there wasn't a blood clot or a hemorrhage in his brain. Tucker was a big man who could handle stallions. The hit he gave Quint would have shook the earth.

People must be arriving at the track by now. The race broadcasters began punctuating the air with announcements. Tucker would return soon, and she still didn't have a plan to keep herself and Quint alive.

He stirred and groaned. Her chest expanded with relief. "Quint?"

He shook his head. "What happened?"

"Tucker clocked you with his gun. We're stuck in this barn and he's going to come back for me soon. We'll probably both be dead in an hour. That should sum it up."

"Your hands are bleeding. Did he cut you?"

"It's from the rope. I can't get out of the knot."

"Did he hurt you? I'll kill him if he did." His face bloomed red.

"I'm okay. I'm more worried about you."

"I've been in worse scrapes than this."

"Please don't tell me that."

Quint moved against the ropes. "I think they're coming loose."

"Keep trying. I tied you up. I don't know the first thing about how to make a good knot."

"You're a horse vet. You might want to change that." He gave her a slow smile and continued to wrestle with the rope.

"First thing after I save our lives."

"Why don't you let me save our lives? That's my job." He held his hands up, and the rope fell to the ground.

He stood up and stumbled.

"Are you dizzy?" Trepidation replaced the relief she felt when he woke.

"I'm fine. Just a little banged up. We're getting out of

here." He hurried over and untied her hands. She flexed her wrists and tried to get the blood flowing into her fingers again.

He cupped her face, and she stared up into his dark eyes. "I know your mouth is hurting, but I need to kiss you," he said.

She leaned into his kiss and opened her mouth to his. She ignored the protest from the cut on her lip and allowed her tongue to tangle with his.

He pulled back. "More of that later. We need to get to the road."

"I want to get my backpack. I dropped it when you followed me."

"Forget it. If Tucker finds us, he'll kill us for certain." He gripped her hand and tugged.

She stood her ground. "Quint, the notebooks and the computer are in there."

"Darlin', please. I'm begging you to let this go. We'll go to Hank. He can help you figure out the next move. You've been through enough already. I won't be able to watch anything else happen to you. Have some mercy on me."

If she wasn't in love with him before, she was now. His eyes pleaded with her, and she wanted to dive into them. "I think I know the way to end this once and for all. Let me have one more try."

"I'm going to regret this. Let's go." He grabbed her hand, and they ran.

CHAPTER 17

QUINT GRIPPED Cheyenne's hand all the way back to the horse barn. He couldn't let go and risk she would slow down and fall behind. His head spun from the heat and the gash in his skull. He tapped at the wound and grimaced. His fingers came back without blood on them.

They had to stop and hide several times to avoid all the people moving about and getting ready for the races. Horse groomers were hosing down the horses. Jockeys ran to their spots. Even spectators had wandered behind the scenes. If anyone noticed them, they'd be dead. Tucker must have returned to the barn and found it empty by now. His men would be on the lookout.

"Do you see it?" He stopped by the barn.

"Right here." She hauled it out from behind a set of

metal garbage cans. "It must've fallen when I dove. When I saw you, I forgot all about it."

"Where to next?"

"The announcers' booth."

He stifled a groan. "You want to go inside the track? We'll be spotted in seconds."

"It's a chance for my father to have the last word."

He should tell her no. They had what they needed. She didn't have to do what she had planned, but she wanted a chance to make things right for her father. "Don't let go of me for anything. You hear?"

"I owe you so much."

"This isn't about owe." It was about love. He loved her enough to do whatever she asked of him. He'd walk over fire for her. He'd walk away from her too if she told him to.

"Hey, you." A male voice shook the last of his reserve.

"We've got to run." He grabbed her hand and took off. It didn't matter who that voice belonged to. They had been found.

"Wait. Come back." The man chased after them.

The groups of people scattered around might be the one thing to save them. He hoped no one would want to draw so much attention they would fire a gun at them.

They had to cross a small access road and weave their way through the grand stand parking lot. He didn't dare look back to see how close they were being followed. Cheyenne had his hand. That's all that mattered.

His heart pounded in his chest, and his lungs fought the air he tried to bring in, but he kept going.

"Watch out," Cheyenne said.

The driver's door of a silver sedan swung open in his path. He dodged it at the last second. Cheyenne let out a whoosh of air. He glanced over his shoulder. Two men were now on their tails and gaining ground.

"Did that door hit you?"

She shook her head. He kept going.

Spectators in their Sunday best made up of suits in light colors and women in straw hats crowded the entrance into the racetrack. He had no choice but to push past them. People yelled and cursed. Someone called for security.

The last entrance stall on the right was closed to guests. He ran for it and jumped over the turnstile. He slid to a stop and turned for Cheyenne. She ducked under it and scrambled to him. The backpack caught on the metal arm and yanked her back. She pulled it free. He took her hand again, and they were off.

THE ANNOUNCERS' booth was on the fourth floor. They would have to take the steps. Cheyenne pumped her legs to keep up with Quint. The man was as fast as a race horse. The backpack collided with her every step, making running that much harder.

Someone was following them. She couldn't look back to see who it was. She would lose her balance and fall. She kept her eyes on Quint's back. Nothing else mattered.

He shoved open the door to the stairs. Two men raced down the steps right for them.

"Shit." Quint pushed her back into the main area where people bet on the races.

They ran across the promenade to another staircase. He threw his shoulder into the metal door as he pushed on the crash bar. Her hand slipped free, and she tripped. His hands grabbed her arms and pulled her up before her chin collided with the first step.

They pounded the stairs. Their footsteps echoed in the stairwell. The first floor became the second. The door below them banged open.

"There they are," Tucker shouted.

She waited for the gunshots, but nothing came. They were dead if he got close enough to catch them. Quint pushed through the door on the third floor and she followed.

"Where are you going?" This wasn't the way to the announcers' booth.

More people placed bets. Families found their seats. Men and women walked with hands full of food and drink. He pulled her to a small alcove that led to the bathrooms and gripped her shoulders.

"We're splitting up," he said.

"What? No."

"Don't argue with me now. I will throw them off long enough for you to get to that booth. Don't stop. Don't look back. Don't worry about me."

"Where will you be?" The tears blurred the image of his face.

"I will come to the booth as soon as I can. Trust no one. You're going to need to get those announcers out of there and then lock the door."

"How am I supposed to do that without you?" She couldn't finish this without him.

"Do you have any magic tricks in that bag?"

"Just a few supplies. Nothing harrowing."

"How about the catheter needle?" He checked out the opening of the alcove. "Three men are searching for us. Cheyenne, will the needle work?"

"I don't know."

"We have to go." He held her face in his hands as if he was studying her. "Trust me. Run for the steps."

He didn't wait for her to answer. He jumped out onto the promenade. "Hey, fuck heads. This way."

She stepped out of the alcove wanting to go after him. He snaked through the crowd in the direction of those men. He was giving her time to get to the steps.

They were right behind him. He turned on his heel.

A man reached out to grab him. Quint cocked his arm and connected his fist to the man's face. The man threw a kick that sent Quint flying. She stifled a scream.

For a second, she thought about helping him.

But instead, she ran.

CHAPTER 18

Cheyenne shoved open the door to the stairs and climbed for her life. She wanted to go back and help Quint, but she couldn't. He had given her the time she needed to find the announcers' booth. He was giving her the gift of a second chance at life. She would honor that and be as brave as he would be.

She pushed open the door at the fourth-floor landing. Less people gathered around on this floor. The restaurant that faced the track was up here, and that was for special patrons only. Several suites offered views of the track too.

The announcer said Dark Matter owned by Cactus Ranch was on the field. His jockey wore the green and white colors of the ranch.

The announcers' booth was tucked in the far-left corner, giving the broadcasters a good view of the finish line. That was what everyone really cared about.

She tried the door, but it was locked. She rummaged through the backpack and pulled out a syringe. She was going to have to fake the rest. She took a deep breath and knocked. No one answered. She banged again.

And again.

The door swung in. "Who the hell is banging on the damn door? You're making a racket." A tall man with a horseshoe of white hair and jowls over his chin scowled at her.

She shoved him back and kicked the door shut. Her heart pounded in her chest. She stuck the oversized syringe under his neck. He reached for the sky.

"Hey." Another man, younger with black hair, pulled off his headphones and jumped out of his chair. He dove for his phone.

"Don't even think about it, or I will inject your friend, and he'll die." The syringe was empty.

The young one backed up. The race began on the track below.

"Lady, let's talk about this," the old guy said.

"You, start announcing. The security guards will be here in seconds if you don't. And don't say anything suspicious." She needed a few minutes to pull off what she wanted to do.

The young guy dropped in his chair and started announcing.

"Sit." She directed the old man to his chair. She

shrugged off the backpack and tried not to think about what Quint was going through. "Open the top compartment and pull out the computer."

"Holy shit, you're going to blow the place up," the young guy said.

"What is your name?"

"Todd."

"Todd, I'm not going to blow up anything. This isn't about you. I need to get on your PA system. That's it. Go back to announcing."

The old guy held the computer. "Do you want to broadcast your husband's infidelity?"

"If it were only that simple. Who are you?"

"I'm John."

"John, I'm about to piss off a very important person, but it's the only way I can prove my innocence. Now, shut up and let me think."

She needed both hands to pull up the files she wanted. She could simply put the microphone up to the computer after that. She wouldn't stay to hear the files play over the speakers and to everyone in the race-track. She'd run back to Quint. If she could find him.

"Type." She pushed the syringe harder against John's neck.

"I don't want to get involved." He held his hands up.

She pushed harder. The needle pricked his skin. He winced. "I'm really sorry, but you are involved now. If I shove this needle into your skin, it's going to cause an air bubble to get into your blood stream which will travel to your heart and kill you."

"Okay, okay. What do you want me to type?"

She gave him the password and the path to the folder. He clicked on the first file. Her father's voice filled the booth.

Todd's voice picked up speed. The race was coming to an end. He stood and leaned closer to the window. He was engrossed in the horses as they rounded the last turn. "And the winner is…Dark Matter."

It was now or never. "Put the microphone up to the computer."

John gripped her hand. "Are you sure you want to do this? Do you know who you're messing with?"

"I do."

Todd placed the microphone beside the computer. Her father's voice drifted out to the field. She took a deep breath. The cantor of his speech was unmistakable. It was as if he were beside her again. Once her hero, now her ghost.

"*I am injecting your horses with steroids forbidden by the racing commission,*" her father said.

The crowd outside went silent. She had their attention finally.

"*I know that. I want to win each and every race, and you're going to help me,*" Tucker Gray said.

The recording went on from there. She had listened to them all and made copies she sent to an online service for safekeeping. She moved the syringe from John's neck.

"I'm sorry about this, but thank you."

"Lady, you're nuts," Todd said.

"Maybe so." She left.

CHAPTER 19

QUINT SAT on a metal folding chair in a ten by twelve room. The walls were cinder blocks painted green. One small window was dirty and didn't let any light in. A single light bulb hung from the ceiling. The table was chipped and cracked. He couldn't reach it. He was handcuffed.

He had been holding his own with the three guys Tucker sent after them. If it hadn't been for the race-track security guards, he might have put the men down and gotten away.

His only thoughts had been to end those men before they killed him. Cheyenne needed to get to the booth and send her father's words out into the crowd. His confession had been the proof she wanted. He hoped she was able to do what she needed. After today, he would be sent away forever. Tucker would see to that. He owned the police too. Quint would never see Cheyenne again.

It was better this way. He was never very good at changing. She could go on with her life and not be caught up with a man like him who couldn't control his anger.

He only wished he could see her one more time. Touch her once more and tell her the right way how he felt. Not some stupid marriage proposal like a teenage tongue-tied boy. She was never going to marry him anyway. She didn't want a life-long commitment. Not with him.

The metal door swung into the room. Jax Montero walked in wearing a white t-shirt, jeans, and fat grin on his face. "Man, you are one big fuck up." Jax pulled keys out of his pocket and unlocked the cuffs.

"I don't understand." He rubbed his wrists.

Jax shook his head. "You're out of here. Hank took care of it."

"But Tucker Gray has this department in his pocket."

"Not everyone." Jax swung the keys on his finger.

"How did you even know I was here?"

Jax turned and pointed to the door. The vision blurred.

"Hi," Cheyenne said.

"She called us. We got her to safety and located you. It's Tucker Gray that's going away for a long time. Let's get the hell out of here. I want to go spend some time with my wife and kid. You keep messing that up."

"I'm sorry."

"I'm joking. Listen, I know you're struggling with what you did today. I'm telling you to leave that shit behind. You were defending someone you care about. I'd kill anyone who hurt Eden. You're not out of control." Jax smacked him on the back.

"I wasn't going to stop."

"No one expected you to."

"Can we have a minute?" He couldn't take his eyes off Cheyenne.

"Take your time. I'll meet you outside." Jax sauntered out.

"Come here." He held his arms open, and she jumped into them.

Her soft curves eased every fiber in his body. He held her close. He would never let her go again.

"I didn't know what else to do," she said into his shoulder. "I left the booth and didn't know where you were. I overheard someone say a man had been arrested. That's when I called Jax. I hid in the ladies' room until he could get there."

"You are one smart lady."

"I was scared out of my mind."

"Me too."

She eased out of his arms and looked up at him. "Really?"

He laced his fingers through hers. "I didn't care

about me. I was afraid something bad was going to happen to you."

"Thank you for protecting me."

"Cheyenne, I need to say something."

"Can I go first?"

"I really need to get this out." He might lose his nerve if he didn't say it now.

"Go ahead."

"You are the first woman in a very long time to make me feel the way I do. With you, I want to be a better man. But when I was fighting today, I was the same man I've always been and that man is no good for you. I meant what I said to Jax. I would've killed those men to save you. I want you to go on with your life. Without me."

She pulled her hands away and fisted them on her hips. "Are you about done?"

"Yeah." He wanted to hang his head.

"Don't tell me who is good enough for me. I make that decision and no one else. I won't make that mistake twice. I love you for wanting to protect me at all costs. And that's what you were doing today. You aren't an evil man looking to hurt anyone. I know how you are with the horses on your ranch. I know how you are with me. That's not a man who has killing in his heart."

"But—"

"I'm not done."

"Okay, then." The corners of his mouth twitched.

He forced them back down.

"You asked me something and I didn't get a chance to answer you. I would like to do that now."

He took her hands again. "Do you need me to ask again?"

"No. It would be an honor to marry you."

His heart swelled in his chest. "This room isn't the right place for this. Let me ask you somewhere proper."

"I don't care where we are as long as we're together."

"Then let me do this like a man." He eased down on one knee and held her gaze. "Cheyenne, I love you. Will you marry me?"

She pressed her lips to his and lingered there for a moment.

She said the only word he needed to hear.

"Yes."

OTHER BOOKS BY STACEY WILK

The Brotherhood Protectors World

Winter's Last Chance

The Last Betrayal

The Heritage River Series

A Second Chance House

The Bridge Home

The Essence of Whiskey and Tea (coming 2019)

Special Forces: Operation Alpha World

Stage Fright

The Omega Team World

Silent Water

The Gabriel Hunter Series

Welcome to Kata-Tartaroo

Welcome to Bibliotheca

Welcome to Skull Mountain

ABOUT STACEY WILK

Stacey Wilk wrote her first novel in middle school to quiet the characters in her head. It was that or let them out to eat the cannolis and she wasn't sharing her grandfather's Italian pastries.

Many years later her life took an adventurous turn when she gave birth to two different kinds of characters. She often sits in awe of their abilities to make objects fly, make it snow on command, and remain dirty after contact with water. She does share the cannolis with them for fear of having her fingers bit off if she doesn't.

Because of the extraordinary characters in her home instead of in her head, including a king who surfaces after dark and for coffee, she writes novels in multiple genres about family, home, and second chances.

When she's not creating stories in make-believe places, she can be found hanging with the cast members of her house or teaching others how to make make-believe worlds of their own.

Stop by for a visit and make sure to bring some cannolis.

www.staceywilk.com

Or her private Facebook group for her amazing readers –
Stacey's Novel Family https://bit.ly/2FK8Lae

Or her newsletter - https://bit.ly/2A0jEFk

ORIGINAL BROTHERHOOD PROTECTORS SERIES

BY ELLE JAMES

Brotherhood Protectors Series

Montana SEAL (#1)

Bride Protector SEAL (#2)

Montana D-Force (#3)

Cowboy D-Force (#4)

Montana Ranger (#5)

Montana Dog Soldier (#6)

Montana SEAL Daddy (#7)

Montana Ranger's Wedding Vow (#8)

Montana SEAL Undercover Daddy (#9)

Cape Cod SEAL Rescue (#10)

Montana SEAL Friendly Fire (#11)

Montana SEAL's Mail-Order Bride (#12)

Montana Rescue (Sleeper SEAL)

Hot SEAL Salty Dog (SEALs in Paradise)

Brotherhood Protectors Vol 1

ABOUT ELLE JAMES

ELLE JAMES also writing as MYLA JACKSON is a *New York Times* and *USA Today* Bestselling author of books including cowboys, intrigues and paranormal adventures that keep her readers on the edges of their seats. With over eighty works in a variety of sub-genres and lengths she has published with Harlequin, Samhain, Ellora's Cave, Kensington, Cleis Press, and Avon. When she's not at her computer, she's traveling, snow skiing, boating, or riding her ATV, dreaming up new stories. Learn more about Elle James at www.elle-james.com

Website | Facebook | Twitter | GoodReads | Newsletter | BookBub | Amazon

Follow Elle!
www.ellejames.com
ellejames@ellejames.com

 facebook.com/ellejamesauthor
 twitter.com/ElleJamesAuthor